"I want your word you won't print this!"

Cass met her eyes, his jaw tense. Then he went on, "Just for once in your life, act like a woman, not a reporter."

"I act like a woman most of the time," Sian threw back, flushing wildly and resenting his words.

"Do you?" He didn't sound convinced, and his brows arched. "Well, act like one now. Forget that my little bride is in the news. She needs your help. Don't take advantage of her."

"I ought to slap you!" Sian said, seething.

Suddenly he laughed, his face changing and a mocking amusement in his eyes. "I wouldn't advise it. I'm bigger and tougher than you are."

He was a lot of things more than she was, Sian thought. More unscrupulous, more arrogant—and far more armored against love.

CHARLOTTE LAMB began to write "because it was one job I
could do without having to leave the children." Now
writing is her profession. She has had more than forty
Harlequin novels published since 1978. "I love to write,"
she explains, "and it comes very easily to me." She and her
family live in a beautiful old home on the Isle of Man,
between England and Ireland. Charlotte spends eight
hours a day working at her typewriter—and enjoys every
minute of it.

Books by Charlotte Lamb

A VIOLATION
SECRETS

HARLEQUIN PRESENTS

851 —SLEEPING DESIRE
874 —THE BRIDE SAID NO
898 —EXPLOSIVE MEETING
971 —HEAT OF THE NIGHT
987 —LOVE IN THE DARK
1001 —HIDE AND SEEK
1025 —CIRCLE OF FATE
1042 —KISS OF FIRE
1059 —WHIRLWIND
1081 —ECHO OF PASSION
1106 —OUT OF CONTROL

HARLEQUIN ROMANCE

2696—KINGFISHER MORNING
2804—THE HERON QUEST
2950—YOU CAN LOVE A STRANGER

CHARLOTTE LAMB

no more lonely nights

Harlequin Books

TORONTO • NEW YORK • LONDON
AMSTERDAM • PARIS • SYDNEY • HAMBURG
STOCKHOLM • ATHENS • TOKYO • MILAN

Harlequin Presents first edition May 1989
ISBN 0-373-11170-3

Original hardcover edition published in 1988
by Mills & Boon Limited

CHAPTER ONE

SIAN did not have second sight, or she would never have said on the phone to her editor that morning, 'I'm going to have a slow, peaceful drive back to London today and I'll see you at work on Monday. I'm still on holiday, and I am not working this weekend, whatever you say, Leo, so forget it.'

'But you'll driving right by the place,' he had protested in his rational, coaxing fashion. 'It wouldn't take you long.'

'You never give up, do you?' Her voice was wry, affectionate, but firm. She wasn't letting Leo talk her into anything. 'I am on holiday, Leo. I won't cover this wedding for you. Got it? Anyway, I'm in no mood to go to a wedding.'

'I see,' he murmured infuriatingly in a voice loaded with meaning.

'What do you see?' she snapped, which was a mistake, she shouldn't have let him see she picked up the implication.

'Love-life still hurting?' he asked sympathetically, and her teeth met.

'I have to pack. See you.'

She hung up before he could come back with anything else, and stared into space for a moment, fuming. Were they all still gossiping at the paper? She thought they had forgotten it by now; she and Louis were an old item, surely? It was weeks since they had split up, after all, and Sian was sure she

5

was over him. She hadn't thought about him much during her holiday. She had been enjoying herself too much; she hadn't given herself time to brood over past mistakes and she wished Leo hadn't reminded her now. People should have found other things to talk about, but the trouble with having lots of friends, or working in a big organisation, was that people took far too close an interest in your private life and felt quite free to comment on it, either to your face or behind your back. Sian hated being talked about. It put her back up. Her life was her business and nobody else had a right to an opinion about it, she thought, glowering, as she set about packing to go back to London.

It didn't take her long. She hadn't brought much; just jeans and shorts and a lot of cotton shirts and T-shirts. She had long ago learnt how to travel light; travelling was part of her job. She lived with a suitcase ready packed; she never knew when Leo would despatch her to some remote corner of the British Isles. That was part of the fascination of the work; Sian had always been excited by the glamour, the roving, gypsy-like nature of a reporter's life. She would hate to be in an office all day, doing nothing but staring out of the window as the rest of the world went by.

It was really her job that had wrecked her relationship with Louis, of course. She was always going away, spending time in hotels with other men, as he saw it; and when she was around she was often tired, she used up too much energy elsewhere to have much to spare for a man.

She and Louis had begun to argue, then to quarrel. When he started on the 'Choose! Me—or your job!' theme that was more or less it. The affair had died out in one violent explosion on both sides. Now that she had cooled down she could see it from his angle and didn't blame him. No man wanted his woman constantly vanishing, always preoccupied. Louis had known what she should have known, that she was more interested in her work than she was in him.

He was seeing someone else, she had heard lately, and that had stung for a second, but she wouldn't be a dog in a manger about Louis. At the same time, she couldn't herself face getting involved with another man; Louis had taught her that she wasn't yet ready for a serious affair, or to give herself entirely to loving anyone, and that was sad, too; that did worry her.

She felt much happier now, though, after a week sailing at Poole, staying with cousins who lived in a delightful harbour cottage. Sian had been weary and irritable when she'd arrived; but she was returning in a very different mood: tanned and relaxed, her green eyes tranquil, after days of physical hard work and mental rest on sun-dappled water. The weather had been perfect—just enough wind, not too much heat. She had been out every day from dawn to dusk, her blonde hair looped up in a ponytail, her shirt and shorts leaving enough of her figure exposed to give her a glowing tan. It had been just what she needed.

'Thanks for having me, Jen,' she told her cousin as she said goodbye on the harbour road. 'It was wonderful.'

'You look better, anyway,' Jenny said, grinning at her.

'I feel it—and when you and Roger come to London next month, don't forget you're staying with me!'

'We won't,' Roger chimed in drily, and they all laughed. Then Sian got behind the wheel of her little Ford and gave them a final wave before heading towards London.

It was June; the morning was already quite warm by the time Sian reached the New Forest, and she drove with the windows wide open and cool air blowing through her blonde hair which she was wearing loose around her face. She was playing a tape of pop music, watching the way the shadows of trees flickered along the road, her mind vaguely drifting over the holiday, the shopping she must do when she was back in her flat, the excitement of getting back to work on Monday.

As she paused at a crossroads her eye noted the name of a nearby village on the signpost. Crasby? Wasn't that where the big wedding was being held? Sian had never been asked to cover a society occasion before; it wasn't her line of territory, the gossip column usually took care of weddings, but the reporter who should have covered this one had apparently rung in earlier to say she was in hospital after crashing on her way down. Leo always liked to kill two birds with one stone, so he had immediately thought of Sian, who was vaguely in the neighbourhood and could drop in at the church on her way back to London. He would just have to send someone else, thought Sian, driving on between the clustering trees.

The girl in white came running out right in front of the car a moment later, and Sian thought for a flash of time that she was seeing ghosts, then with a jolt of horror that she was going to hit the girl.

Luckily both her reflexes and her brakes were in good working order. She slammed her foot down, and the car came to a rocking halt with a scream of burning tyres.

Sian sat, gripping the wheel, for an instant, then she went white, and a second later bright, angry red.

'Are you crazy?' she yelled, leaning out of the window.

'Sorry, I'm sorry,' babbled the girl, stumbling round the car to the other window.

Sian's blonde head followed her movements, her green eyes dilated and incredulous. She had had her eyes open for wild ponies or deer. All along the road there were signs warning drivers of their presence—but there were none telling you to beware of brides! The last thing Sian had been expecting to see was a bride in full regalia: an extravagantly romantic dress of foaming white satin and lace, a flowing veil thrown back from the face over a high head-dress of pearls and tiny white flowers, a be-ribboned bouquet of white roses and pink carnations clutched in the hand which had gripped the window-frame of the car.

'I didn't mean to startle you, and I am sorry, but please . . . could you give me a lift? It is urgent,' the bride said breathlessly.

'Don't tell me the bridal car didn't arrive,' Sian said, unable to stay angry for long, and beginning to smile as she leaned over to open the passenger door. 'Hop in, then.'

The bride bundled herself and all her layers of satin and lace into the seat with some difficulty, while Sian watched with amusement. The bride looked at her, not smiling back. Sian might find it funny, but obviously she couldn't see the funny side of her predicament at the moment. In fact, there was a look of panic in her face, and Sian felt sorry for having laughed.

'Please...' the bride began, and Sian nodded.

'Don't worry, I'll get you there on time,' she soothed. 'And I'm sure the groom will wait. Did you think of ringing the church to say you'd be late?' And where was the bride's father, come to that? she thought curiously, and then saw it had been a mistake to mention the groom. The bride was looking almost faint.

'Can we go, please? I'm sorry to rush you but...'

'Not at all,' said Sian quickly, starting the engine again. 'Can you direct me? Where's the church? I'm a stranger around here—isn't it always the way?'

The bride didn't answer for a second, then she said huskily, 'Where are *you* going?'

'Back to London—I've been down here on holiday, sailing.' Sian sat waiting, her hands on the wheel, the engine running, watching the other girl. 'So? Where do I go?' she prompted when the bride just bit her lip and said nothing.

'London,' whispered the bride. Sian did a double-take, doubting her own ears.

'Sorry?'

'London's fine for me, too,' repeated the other with a self-conscious look, her eyes not meeting Sian's.

That was when Sian's brain got to work on the situation and she remembered Leo's call, the signpost she had noticed a few moments earlier. Of course, on a Saturday a lot of people got married, some churches had a constant stream of brides coming and going, but the coincidence was enough to make Sian sit up, alert and watchful.

'London? You're sure you want to go to London?' she asked, and the dark girl nodded fiercely.

'Yes, please, I've got to get away before...'

'Before?' Sian's green eyes narrowed to catlike slits of comprehension. 'Before someone catches up with you?'

The dark girl swallowed. 'So please can we drive on?' she muttered. Sian obeyed, putting her foot down on the accelerator. The car shot forward with a happy roar.

'Why didn't you change out of the wedding dress before you left?' Sian asked curiously, and the girl sighed.

'I didn't think, I just climbed out of the window.'

'Out of the window?' repeated Sian incredulously.

'We live in a bungalow—at least, my father does, and he was at the front, watching out for the car. I climbed out of my bedroom window.'

'Why didn't you just tell your father that you couldn't go through with it?'

The bride groaned. 'I've never been able to talk to Dad. If my Mum hadn't died I might have told her, but Dad was so pleased that I was marrying Cass...' She broke off, and Sian sat very still as she drove, her brain clicking wildly.

She was right, it had to be *him*, William Cassidy. Everyone called him Cass, especially the newspapers, and he was often in the news because he headed a successful electronics firm with a very active public relations department who managed to keep his name and the firm's products firmly in the public eye. Sian didn't work on the gossip pages, she was strictly a news reporter, but she had vaguely known of his surprise engagement and rapid wedding. Wasn't he marrying his secretary, or a typist, or something? A very ordinary girl, anyway; that had excited the gossip columnists.

'I'm Sian, by the way,' she said carefully. 'What's your name?'

'Annette.'

Sian couldn't recall that name, but then she hadn't looked at the bride's name too closely. She hadn't been sufficiently interested except to give the story her usual professional glance. One had to keep up with all the news in the paper. Sometimes two stories dovetailed unexpectedly, and if you didn't know about the other one you might miss something vital. She probably wouldn't have connected this girl with William Cassidy, for instance, if Leo hadn't rung her earlier that morning. He had put the wedding into her mind, alerting her.

'It's very kind of you to do this,' the other girl said shyly. 'I realise it must seem a bit odd, but I just knew I couldn't go through with it. All of a sudden I had to get away. Every time I tried to talk to Cass or to Dad the words didn't come out right. They make me feel...helpless.'

Sian slowed as they approached a pull-off for picnicking, a grassy little glade opening from a parking area, but surrounded by trees. The other girl looked startled as Sian drove off the road.

'What's wrong? Why are you stopping?'

'You don't want to drive through London like that, do you? I think we're much the same size. I've got a suitcase in the back, I'll lend you some clothes to change into, if you like.'

'Oh,' Annette said, flushing. 'Oh, thanks, that's very...'

Sian parked and turned off the engine, but before she fished out her case she looked round at the other girl, her face serious. Sian was a slightly built girl of around twenty-five, with classical features and a cool, self-contained air. She gave the impression of having herself and her world well under control, but that wasn't altogether accurate. Sian so far hadn't managed to make her two lives fit, the personal and the professional. At the moment she would prefer to forget any idea of having a private life, anyway. She wasn't risking the minefield of a love affair again for a long, long time, and she looked at Annette with wry sympathy.

'Love's tough to handle, isn't it?'

Tears came into the other girl's brown eyes and Sian looked away, not sure what to say to her.

Abruptly, she muttered, 'Look, I know this isn't any of my business, but I've got to stick my neck out. Are you sure you know what you're doing? I mean, it is quite common for a bride to panic on her wedding day, or so I'm told.' She laughed without real humour. 'Personally, I wouldn't know, of course, I've never got that far, but I've often heard of brides suddenly feeling they've made a mistake. It's a big decision; scary, too, I'd imagine, but once you had gone through with it maybe you would realise it really was what you wanted, after all.'

'No, that's just it,' burst out the other girl. 'It never was.'

Sian looked sharply at her. 'Never?'

'No.' Annette was very flushed, her tearful eyes enormous. 'He asked me and I don't even remember saying yes, but suddenly we were engaged and I felt like someone who had got caught up by something, a tornado, maybe, blowing me away. It all happened too fast and my father was so thrilled. Cass is . . . well, the man I'm marrying is rich, he can give me so much. Dad isn't after the money, honestly, but he was pleased that I was going to be looked after. Dad isn't very strong; his health is bad and since my mother died we've only had each other, there are no other relatives. Dad was afraid he would die and I'd be alone, so he sort of jumped at Cass, I'm afraid.'

'But you must have liked . . . the man you're engaged to,' Sian suggested with care.

Annette bit her lip. 'When I met him there was someone else, but he went away. He misunderstood, he thought I preferred Cass, but I didn't—only, when Rick, the other man, left, I was miserable, and Cass was there, and I didn't care about anything. It didn't seem to matter whether I married Cass or not for a long time.'

A great light had dawned on Sian. There was someone else; a man Annette preferred, was in love with, a younger man, Sian suspected, and probably one without much money if he was so jealous of William Cassidy.

'And then this morning he rang me,' Annette whispered, her voice thick with choked tears.

'He?'

'Rick. This other man.'

'What did he say?'

The tears were running down Annette's face now. 'That he hoped I'd be happy, but Cass could never love me the way he did. He sounded so unhappy, then he rang off in the middle of saying something, and I got scared. What if he does something stupid? He wouldn't, would he?'

She looked beseechingly at Sian, who soothed her. 'I'm sure he won't.' Shrewdly, Sian asked, 'Does he live in London?'

Startled, Annette nodded. 'However did you guess that?'

'It wasn't difficult,' Sian said, amused. 'But you know, you can't just leave your bridegroom standing at the altar.' Her green eyes focused commandingly on the other girl's face. 'You must ring the church and explain. We'll stop at the next telephone box we see.'

Annette sighed heavily, but agreed. Sian smiled at her, then got out her suitcase, opened it and hunted for a clean pair of jeans and a clean shirt. Annette changed among the crowding trees; it took her quite a while, and Sian suspected she was crying too much to be deft-fingered, but she left the girl alone while she herself thought through what she should do. Heaven had dropped a once-in-a-lifetime scoop into her lap. No reporter worth her salt could possibly let it get away. If she didn't report this story, sooner or later the rest of the press would get on to it. William Cassidy was news. For all Sian knew, the press had already got the story—had Annette been missed yet? Had her father raised the alarm?

Annette came out of the trees, carrying her gown and veil over her arm, her white shoes clutched in one hand. She now looked very ordinary: a slim, athletic girl in jeans and a shirt. Sian wondered curiously what William Cassidy had fallen for in her. She was a nice enough girl and quite pretty, but there was nothing special about her.

Sian grimaced to herself as she thought that although the eyes of love were always blind to faults, they saw what everyone else had missed—the uniqueness of one human being.

As they drove on, Sian said, 'Annette, I ought to tell you. I'm a journalist, and I was actually asked to cover your wedding.'

'Oh, really? What a coincidence,' Annette murmured, staring out of the window, chewing on her lower lip. Her voice was abstracted—had she really heard? Sian wondered, preparing to repeat her admission.

Annette broke in on her before she could get another word out. 'Oh, look,' she said, pointing. 'A telephone.'

They were passing through a small village street; the telephone was outside a shop and Sian pulled up just beyond it. Annette sat, staring, her pale face a battleground.

'I can't,' she said. 'He might come to the phone. I couldn't talk to him, really. He's so . . . sometimes Cass scares me, he's like lightning—you know the way it seems to be tearing the sky up? Blinding light, and a terrible violence. Cass is like that. He can be very polite and sweet, but underneath you always feel there's this possible violence. Rick's ordinary, like me, we suit each other because we're the same. Rick isn't rich, you know, he's a salesman. He used to work for Cass, but he left when... when he walked out on me. He could see Cass liked me, at once.' She turned big, puzzled eyes on Sian. 'Why does he, though? I've never been able to understand that. Why does he want me? I'm not from his sort of class. And he's had so many really beautiful women in his life. He didn't marry any of them—so why me?'

'It isn't his feelings that matter, it's yours,' Sian said patiently. 'So why don't you just ring your home and tell your Dad? Or ring the church and tell the Vicar? You must do something, Annette. You can't leave them all in a state of utter ignorance. They might get the police.'

'The police?' Annette looked horrified. 'I never thought...'

'I can see you didn't, but it's time you did. Go and ring. Put their minds at rest.'

Annette got out of the car slowly, then stayed there, wringing her hands in a frantic way. 'I can't talk to them,' she wailed, looking at Sian pleadingly. 'I'm so scared. They'll be so angry. They'll shout. Cass... no, I couldn't talk to Cass. And Dad... he might cry, that would be worse. He'll be so upset, and Cass will be so angry. I can't do it. Please, Sian.'

Sian didn't get it for a second, then she shook her head with vehemence. 'Oh, no, I'm not doing it for you. This is up to you. You got yourself into this muddle, you should get yourself out. You must handle your own life, Annette, and now is a good time to start.'

She might have saved her breath. Annette got back into the car and cried, and Sian began to see that under that helpless exterior there was something tenacious: a weakness that was a sort of strength because it made other people take control of her life for her, and saved her the trouble. Annette was used to that—expected it, probably demanded it. Was that why William Cassidy proposed to her?

'What time was the wedding?' Sian asked in the end, looking at her watch.

'Eleven-thirty,' said Annette, and Sian's eyes widened. It was still only eleven-fifteen; she had somehow believed that Annette had run away just seconds before the wedding began.

'OK, where do I ring?' she asked, and Annette told her the name of the church. She didn't know the number, but Sian got it from directory enquiries. First, though, she rang her paper and spoke to Leo, who was at once excited.

'You aren't kidding?'

'Now why should I?'

'She ran out of the forest right under your car? In all her bridal get-up? Would you credit it?' He laughed and Sian made a face he couldn't see. Typical of a man, not to mention an editor. Leo was over-sophisticated, cynical. He wasn't here; he couldn't see Annette's face. Annette wasn't real to him, none of the stories they printed were; they were just journalistic fiction unattached to real human beings.

'She's an unhappy girl,' Sian told him. There was real blood in Annette's veins, real tears on her cheeks.

'Poor kid,' said Leo. 'I'll switch you through to a copy-typist and I'll check that we can get pictures from the locals. I think there's an agency man down there; if we could get his pictures exclusively...'

'Just put me through to copy, would you?' said Sian impatiently. Sometimes Leo annoyed her.

She rapidly gave a copy-typist a rough story which the subs would no doubt put into better shape, then rang the church and left a message with a man who sounded vague and bewildered.

'The bride won't be here? I don't understand.'

'She has changed her mind, she's sorry, she's gone to London,' said Sian.

'Changed her mind?'

'Yes, she can't go through with the wedding—will you please tell Mr Cassidy she's very sorry.'

'Mr Cassidy? He's here.'

Alarmed, Sian said, 'Well, just tell him,' but the other man had suddenly gone. She heard his voice at a distance, speaking to someone else; then, before Sian could put the phone down, another voice came on the line, a hard, authoritative voice which made Sian stiffen.

'Who *is* that?' it demanded curtly.

'You don't know me, I'm ringing for Annette.' Sian was getting nervous now; that voice was daunting, she could see why Annette had run away.

'Where is she? Let me speak to her,' he grated.

'She's too upset to talk,' Sian hurriedly improvised. 'She asked me to let you know that she's very

sorry, she knows it is a bit late to do this, but she
has realised she can't go through with the wedding.'

'What the hell are you talking about? Where is
she? Put her on the line—or is this some sort of
hoax? Are you playing damn silly games with me,
whoever you are?'

'No, of course not.' Even granting that he must
be shaken, distraught, Sian wasn't putting up with
being bullied and spoken to in that tone of voice.
'I've given you the message, I must go now. Annette
is very sorry, Mr Cassidy.'

'Look, damn you——' he burst out, but she was
already putting down the phone. As she turned back
to the car she saw Annette drying her eyes and
looking at herself in the car wing-mirror.

'You look fine,' she told her, getting behind the
wheel. 'I can lend you some make-up, if you like.'

'Thanks,' Annette said, then asked huskily, 'Did
you . . . ?'

'I rang the church, yes, and spoke to your bridegroom himself.'

The other girl went crimson, then white. 'Cass?
What did he say? Was he very angry?'

Sian gave her a dry glance—did she know anything about the man at all? She was a human jel-
lyfish, drifting on seas she didn't comprehend.

'I think you could say that.'

The sarcasm made Annette bite her lip again,
looking like an unhappy schoolgirl. 'I knew he
would be, that was why I couldn't speak to him
myself.' She took the cosmetic bag Sian handed her.
'You're very kind, thank you.' Sian started the car
again and drove off while Annette was doing

wonders to her face with the various cosmetics she fished out of the bag.

'One thing puzzles me,' said Sian as she drove. 'Why on earth were you carrying your bouquet and wearing your veil?'

'I don't know,' Annette said, starting to giggle. 'I just ran and didn't stop to think. I was holding the bouquet, you see. My father went off and I stood looking in the mirror at myself. I was ready to leave, then suddenly I knew I couldn't, so I climbed out of the window and started running through the forest.'

'Running away isn't usually the right way to deal with things,' Sian said quite gently, although she was beginning to feel that Annette needed a few home truths. She was amazingly immature for someone of her age; more an adolescent than a woman. What on earth had William Cassidy seen in her?

'Where shall I drop you in London?' she asked some time later, and Annette came out of a dazed silence to give her an address. 'Is that where your Rick lives?' Sian asked, and saw by Annette's blush that she was right. How would William Cassidy's rival feel about the runaway bride appearing on his doorstep? Was he seriously in love with her, or had he been a little relieved at losing her to another man? But it wasn't Sian's business; once she dropped Annette off she could forget about the whole sorry muddle. That would be quite a relief, she decided, putting her foot down on the accelerator.

*   *   *

Her flat seemed tranquil; a haven of solitude. Sian unpacked, had a bath, sat and watched TV and ignored the phone which kept ringing. She knew who it was—Leo, trying to get an update on the William Cassidy story. Leo would want to hear the inside details: where the bride had bolted to and with whom—but he wasn't getting any of that from Sian. She had given him a scoop as it was; the other papers would have got on to the cancelled wedding later, but her paper would have it in type with pictures, with any luck. They might even get an exclusive; it depended how many media people had been at the wedding.

The phone began to ring again. When it had stopped, she switched it on to the answering machine, made herself some cocoa and went to bed, amused by Leo's persistence. Over the next half-hour she heard the phone start to ring again and again, although each time it cut out as the machine came into operation. How many messages was Leo leaving her? she wondered sleepily, on the edge of oblivion.

It had been a very tiring day; a lot had happened, and she was asleep before long. The next thing she knew was that someone was hammering on her door. Sian came awake with a violent start and fell out of bed, literally. She didn't hurt herself, but she was dazed for a moment, and lay there listening in disbelief to the reverberations of someone's fist hitting the solid wood of her front door. She had a doorbell. He rang that, too, at the same time.

Leo? she thought incredulously, but knew it wasn't. Her intuition told her that her angry visitor could only be one man, but surely Leo hadn't given him her address? That was against the rules. Editors never gave out reporters' names and addresses, to anyone.

Unless, of course, they had a lot of clout, and used it ruthlessly! She got to her feet and switched on the light. Grabbing up her filmy white négligé, she gave herself a rapid glance in the bedroom mirror; her blonde hair was ruffled, her skin pale, her green eyes startled. She looked as nervous as she felt, but there was nothing she could do about that, so she put on her négligé and hurried to the door.

As soon as she began to open it a body thrust it wider and she fell back, staring at the man who confronted her.

She had had no real idea what William Cassidy looked like, but she knew at once that it was him. It couldn't be anyone else. This was a very angry man and a very tall one, with a face full of violence, in odd juxtaposition to the sort of sleek tailoring associated with society weddings: morning suit, white carnation in the buttonhole, dove-grey silk tie, smooth shirt.

'Where is she?' he asked in a voice hoarse with rage, and Sian nerved herself to defy him.

CHAPTER TWO

'I CAN'T tell you that!' Sian began. William Cassidy kicked the front door shut without taking his eyes off her. The slam made her jump, her wide eyes wary.

'Oh, yes, you will,' he assured her, and she felt the hairs on the back of her neck bristling.

'Don't you threaten me! I gave Annette my word not to tell anyone where she is, and I'm going to keep my word.'

The force of her voice made his eyes narrow; for the first time he really looked at her. She saw a glitter of curiosity in those cold grey eyes. He coolly looked her up and down, and she seethed with resentment over the expression on his hard face.

'How admirable,' he drawled. 'You must be a very unusual reporter—the others of your trade I've met haven't had the same scruples.'

She wished she could deny the slur on her profession, but, she thought with a grimace, she knew some of her colleagues a little too well.

'Yes, well, sorry about that, Mr Cassidy, but we aren't all out of the same box.'

His brows arched. 'No? But it seems your so-called scruples didn't stop you taking advantage of Annette's confidences. Your paper will be printing the story tomorrow. Your editor wouldn't let me see the copy, but he admitted enough to make it clear that you used Annette ruthlessly.'

Sian went red. 'I can understand why you're angry.'

'Oh, can you?' he broke in bitingly, and she bit her lip.

'How did you find out about me?' she asked suddenly, and he leaned on her front door to consider her drily.

'The local journalist told me your paper had rung his office, who rang him at the church. When I tried to talk to your editor on the phone I got nowhere, so I drove up to London myself to shake your address out of him.'

'I'm sorry you've gone to all this trouble, but I'm not telling you where Annette is. You've wasted your time,' Sian said uneasily, hoping he was going to admit defeat and go. She wasn't too optimistic, though; he didn't have the face of a man who easily admitted defeat, and she could well understand why Annette had fled him. This was very disturbing material for any woman to work with; Sian was not easily daunted by men, but for him she made an exception. She found him quite unnerving.

'You don't understand yet——' he began, but she interrupted, shaking her head.

'I do, I assure you! I know men find it hard to forgive a blow to their ego.'

'Oh, you know that, do you?' He eyed her drily. 'And although I've only known you a short time, Miss Christian, I get the feeling you have given quite a few men a blow to the ego.' He watched the surprise and then the resentment show in her green eyes, but before she could say anything else he shrugged his powerful shoulders and said crisply, 'This is just wasting time. Look, Miss Christian, it's essential that I find Annette. Her father had a heart attack when he discovered she had run away.'

Sian gave a sharp gasp, and stared at him. Was he telling the truth?

He read her expression and smiled coldly. 'If you want to check that statement, I can give you the name of the hospital and the ward he's in!'

'Poor Annette,' Sian murmured, frowning, believing him then. 'Is it serious?'

William Cassidy hesitated, his brows drawn. 'I'm no doctor,' he said at last, and Sian watched him, guessing that he knew more than he was saying. 'Now, can I have Annette's address?' he demanded.

She thought quickly. 'I promised not to tell you.'

'Circumstances have changed, surely?' he snapped, and she nodded.

'I know, but I can still keep my word if I take you there rather than tell you, and anyway, I think it would make it easier for Annette if I was there when she heard the news. This is going to be a real blow for her.'

His face was sombre. 'I'm afraid it is, they were very close. There are no other relatives, and Lewis, her father, has aggravated his condition by fretting over Annette being left alone when he's gone.'

Sian's intuition leapt, and she looked hard at him. 'You mean, this heart condition hasn't suddenly shown itself? He's been ill for a long time?'

William Cassidy nodded, then said impatiently, 'Look, if you're taking me there, will you get dressed at once? There's no time to be lost.'

'I won't be two minutes,' she promised, hurrying back to her bedroom. She flung on the first clothes she found; pale blue denim trousers and a loose pink top which she belted at the waist with a silvery chain. She didn't bother to put on make-up, and simply knotted her blonde hair at the nape with a blue ribbon. In the mirror her face was oddly alive—green eyes very bright, skin flushed. That was strange, because she should have been sleepy or pale; she had been woken out of deep sleep and given a series of shocks. She didn't have time to investigate her own strange reactions, though. She ran back down the hall and found William Cassidy waiting at the door.

He hustled her out of the flat, but managed at the same time to run a glance over her and make her prickle with aggression. That cool, go-to-hell look of his made her want to hit him. She might not be dressed to kill, she might even look very flustered, but what did he expect? He had asked her to hurry, or she would have taken more trouble with how she looked. What business was it of his, anyway? Sian didn't care what he thought of how she looked.

He had a car waiting outside; in the yellowish gleam of the street lamps she admired the sleek limousine, a classy dark blue shade on the chassis, the upholstery a power-blue leather. As he helped her into the passenger seat, she thought grimly that she could very soon get used to travelling in this luxury. Her body sank into the deep upholstery and she leaned back, staring up at the dark sky above London. If Annette was asleep, her awakening was going to be painful. Sian sighed. This had been quite a day for both of them, and what would the next day bring—for Annette, at least?

William Cassidy slid in beside her and the engine purred into life. When it moved off the car seemed to glide, but at speed; she felt as if they were flying, and watched his hands on the wheel with hypnotised fascination. What did it feel like to have this beautiful machine throbbing in your hands? Sian had to admit he handled it with cool mastery, those long-fingered hands relaxed even though he was driving fast at times on the empty city roads. Most of London was asleep; she almost felt that the two of them were the only ones awake, silent and alone together in their entranced, mysterious city.

Once William Cassidy had found the suburb to which she had taken Annette, Sian had to guide him, from memory, to the street itself. When they pulled up outside the small, terraced yellow-brick house, he leaned on the wheel, his dark head lowered as he stared with a frown.

'You brought her here? Why here?'

'That's for Annette to tell you.' She wondered how much he knew or guessed about Annette's motive in running away, about his rival. Was he going to get another shock when he found out? There was no reason why she should find that upsetting, but she did, oddly enough. So far she hadn't got the impression that William Cassidy was vulnerable or easily hurt, but he was a man and had feelings, and Sian bit her lip as he got out of the car.

She joined him on the pavement, grabbing his arm. 'Break it gently, won't you?' she pleaded. He looked down at her in surprise, as if he had already forgotten who she was, then smiled suddenly.

'Of course I will. Don't worry. I care about her, you know.'

Sian felt an odd little stab right below the ribs, an inexplicable pain which made her frown as she followed him up the narrow little pathway to the front door, shivering in the cold night air. It was a very clear night, the stars were white fire and very close, you could almost touch them, but they would burn your fingers if you did, she thought crazily, trying to bury the memory of that strange, worrying jab of pain. She had only just met William Cassidy; he was nothing to her, so why should she be concerned about his feelings for anyone else?

'Cold?' he asked her then, ringing the front-door bell. 'I've got an overcoat in the car, I'll get it for you.'

He went back with quick, lithe steps while lights came on in the rooms upstairs, and voices sounded—anxious, puzzled, startled voices. Sian thought she picked up the note of Annette's voice, then William Cassidy came back with a smooth black cashmere overcoat which he draped casually around her shoulders. She was far shorter than he was, and it hung down almost to her feet, but it was very warm and she snuggled into it with a sigh of gratitude.

'Thank you.'

He looked down at her, then suddenly grinned. 'If you could see yourself...' His amusement died as the front door opened and a young man faced them, defiant and pale.

'Wesley?' William Cassidy looked utterly taken aback, and the other man squared himself up, as if expecting to have to fight.

'You aren't taking her back. She won't see you,' he said, in a deep yet not quite steady voice. He was much closer to Annette's age, maybe in his early twenties, thought Sian, amazed that Annette could prefer this smooth-faced boy with the very ordinary looks to someone as impressive as William Cassidy. It wasn't simply that Cass had more money, or the sort of power that could confer glamour on a man, but he was unquestionably the better-looking of the two. Cass was bigger, taller, with a more forceful and commanding face; his features were powerful yet elegant, with razor-cut bones, and hypnotic grey eyes.

Rick, on the other hand, was fair and a little ungainly, with worried blue eyes and a firmly moulded mouth. Why did Annette care so much for him? But then, why did any woman fall in love? You couldn't compute it, it didn't respond to logic or common sense; it was just a runaway emotion that took its victim headlong into passion, and Sian envied Annette, if she was truthful. She had never felt like that for anyone. If she had cared more for Louis, she wouldn't have let her job keep them apart. She wouldn't have let anything keep them apart. She had liked him, but she hadn't been mad enough about him to abandon everything else, the way Annette just had.

'I'm afraid I've got bad news for her,' Cass said in a low voice, and Rick Wesley frowned, uncertain yet disturbed.

'Bad news?' He kept his voice down, glancing over his shoulder. No doubt Annette was hovering there, out of sight but within earshot.

'Her father had a heart attack. He's in hospital, in intensive care.' William Cassidy's voice was still subdued, and Rick leant towards him to hear, his face very white.

'Oh, my God, no!'

'I'm afraid so.' Cass watched the younger man with a frowning compassion. 'Will you tell her or...'

'She's upset already. She looked out of the window and saw it was you. How can I tell her this?' Rick made a gesture as if he were wringing his hands, and shivered. He was in pyjamas and dressing-gown, his bare feet pushed into slippers, his hair untidy. Sian watched and thought how young he looked, how helpless. He didn't have a clue how to deal with this crisis.

'What do I say?' he asked Cass, who wryly glanced sideways at Sian.

'Do you think you might...?'

'Yes, I'll tell her,' she agreed, although she thought Annette might prefer to hear this from Rick. As they all began to enter the house, Annette herself appeared on the stairs, very pale in a green cotton wrap, her hand holding the neck of it, her eyes big and glazed with fear and suspense.

'You promised not to tell him where I was,' she accused Sian huskily, looking at her in reproach.

'I'm sorry, Annette, I had to!' Sian said, going towards her.

The other girl backed away, shaking her head. 'What did he pay you? I thought I could trust you. It just shows, you should never trust anybody!'

Sian put out her hand, her eyes steadily fixed on Annette's face. 'I've got to talk to you, Annette.

Come down.' She looked round. 'Is there some-where where we can talk, Rick?'

'I don't want to talk to you...' Annette broke off, frowning. 'Talk about what? What are you...'

Sian's green eyes went back to her.

Annette's intake of air was audible. 'What is it?' She stared down into Sian's face and grew intensely pale. 'My father?' The leap of intuition did not surprise Sian somehow. Gently, she told Annette the truth and the other girl closed her eyes, giving a sharp cry of anguish.

'My fault, it's all my fault—he's going to die, because of me!'

'No,' Sian said quickly, but Cass spoke first, his voice insistent.

'His heart has been bad for the past year, Annette. It's amazing that he hasn't had a serious attack before. You can't blame yourself, it isn't your fault.'

Sian watched him through her lashes; his face was gentle now, all the rage gone. He must love Annette deeply. As he had admitted, he really cared about her, even though she had hurt him badly by deserting him at the very altar for another man. Only a very deep love could forgive such a betrayal. William Cassidy must be quite a man, Sian wryly decided. Couldn't Annette see that?

Annette was crying now, her hands over her face. Sian moved towards her, but Rick got there first, putting his arms round the girl's slim, shaking body. He led her back up the stairs, murmuring to her. Sian heard a door close, then Rick came back to the top of the stairs and looked down.

'She's getting dressed. I'll dress, too, and come with you, if that's OK.' His tone was defiant, and his eyes said that even if it wasn't OK with William Cassidy he was coming anyway.

'We'll wait outside in my car,' Cass said without any other comment.

Back in the warmth and comfort of the limousine, Sian shed the overcoat, handing it back to him. 'Thank you. What a gorgeous coat it is! Pure cashmere, isn't it?'

He took it absent-mindedly. 'What? Oh, yes, I think it is.' Clearly, he didn't care, and he settled back into his own seat a moment later, tapping his long fingers on the wheel, looking up at the lighted windows of the little house. 'I didn't realise she had run to Wesley,' he said, almost to himself. 'In fact, I'd no idea that they were ever close.' He shot Sian a look, frowning, his grey eyes probing her face. 'She told you about him? I gather you knew.'

'I think she was dating him before she started seeing you.'

He nodded, his mouth a firm line, curiosity in his eyes.

'In fact,' Sian decided to add, 'I gathered that you scared him away—he felt he couldn't compete. As you see, he doesn't have your...' She paused to find the right word, and ended, 'Advantages.'

He looked round at the small house. 'Is this his place or...?'

'His parents live here,' Sian told him.

'She poured it all out to you, did she?' He was looking angry again, his facial bones tight. 'Or did you coax her to confide all her secrets? Am I going to read all about it in tomorrow's paper?'

Sian was flushed, her green eyes hectic and defiant. 'It's my...'

'Job!' he finished for her with a bite that made her stiffen. 'Excuse yourself with that corny old line, if you like, but don't ask me to accept it, because I don't. Annette didn't know what she was doing when she talked so much. If she had realised you were a journalist...'

'I told her!'

That stopped him in his tracks for a minute; he stared at her with dislike, then shrugged. 'Maybe you did and she didn't realise what that would mean. I can't believe she wanted her private life splashed all over the newspapers.'

Sian knew he was probably right; Annette had not been in a condition to know what might happen if she confided so openly in a total stranger. She hadn't really taken in what Sian said about her job, she hadn't been listening.

'It made rather a romantic little story,' she said drily, knowing he would hate what she was going to say, but determined to say it. 'Annette's such a nice, ordinary girl, and she chose not to be Cinderella to your Prince Charming—she ran away from the ball back to her nice, ordinary young man. You may not find that charming, but a lot of readers will.'

The front door opened and they both watched as Annette appeared with Rick hovering protectively at her elbow. She was wearing a warm anorak under which Sian recognised the clothes she had lent her. Had Rick lent her the anorak?

'I know you must have been badly hit, but try to understand,' she said hurriedly to William

Cassidy, who turned a blank face to her and didn't answer.

Sian realised it was early for him to begin to get over the first blow of finding out that Annette had run away from him, but this was no time for him to say anything to Annette. She would have enough problems coping with guilt over her father's heart attack. Sian had learnt during their drive up from the New Forest to London just how close father and daughter were, how attached Annette was to her father, and how much he, in turn, cared about her.

'She'll blame herself,' Sian told William Cassidy as Annette and Rick came towards the car. 'She mustn't; it could haunt her for the rest of her life if her father dies now. Don't make it harder for her.'

'Damn you, what makes you think I will?' he muttered furiously, then got out of the car to greet the other two. A moment later they were in the rear seats and the limousine was sliding away from the kerb. There were still lights on in the little terraced house; no doubt Rick's parents were up now and distressed over the events of the past few hours.

Nothing was said on the long drive back, along the motorway, passing very few cars, the wide road unwinding in a strange yellow glare while overhead the starlit sky had a melancholy beauty. Sian leaned back and listened to the brooding silence in the car. Beside her Cass drove without a flicker of expression on his lean face; his hands resting lightly on the wheel, his gaze fixed always ahead. In the back, Annette seemed half asleep, but every now and then she made a sound which wasn't quite a sob, yet wasn't ordinary breathing either. Each time Sian felt Rick stir, felt him move, tightening his hold on her, half murmuring to her.

It was not a comfortable drive, and Sian was relieved to see the dark bulk of the New Forest looming up. It had certainly never entered her head when she set out from here this morning that she was going to be driving back again quite so soon. It was probably just as well that human beings couldn't see into the future.

Cass swung the car round a corner suddenly, and Sian leaned forward to glimpse a hospital just ahead of them at the end of a drive. It blazed with lights even at this hour; she saw an ambulance standing on a forecourt, saw two nurses in dark capes going through swing doors, their white uniforms shown up by the light from a window.

'Will they let me see him?' Annette suddenly whispered.

'You may have to wait a while,' Cass told her quite kindly, and she gave another of those funny little sobs.

'He'll be OK,' Rick muttered, his arm round her and his chin on her hair. 'You'll see. They can do wonders these days.'

Cass pulled up on the hospital drive outside a double-doored entrance. 'I'll go and park—you had better get out here,' he said, and they all began to get out. Annette didn't really need Sian, but somehow Sian was reluctant to leave her. She had become inextricably involved in this; she felt she had to stay, see it through. Annette had Rick to lean on for the moment, but she might still need another woman around, especially as Cass was there, too. The two men weren't overtly hostile, but on the other hand they had a guarded wariness which came close to out-and-out hostility. At any moment they could start acting belligerently, and that was the last thing Annette needed. It would help if Sian was there to stop any trouble before it became serious.

Cass was wrong; Annette did not have to wait to see her father. As soon as they arrived she was taken upstairs to the ward in which he lay, while Rick and Sian sat in a glass-walled waiting-room. When Cass joined them he asked if either of them wanted a drink of coffee or tea.

Rick shook his head, his face averted, but Sian said she wouldn't say no to some coffee—it would help her to stay awake.

'I'll show you where the machine is,' Cass said, turning on his heel, and she followed him along the corridor. When he reached the vending machine he just leaned on the wall beside it, his grey eyes sharp as he watched her read the instructions.

'I was so preoccupied with Annette that it didn't impinge on me that you had somehow managed to stay with us,' he said coolly. 'Let me warn you, if you have some notion of getting further copy out of this, you're mistaken. You've taken advantage of Annette once, you aren't doing it again while I'm around.'

Sian ignored that, hunting for a coin in her purse. His hand suddenly shot out and grabbed her wrist.

'Do you hear?' he snarled, and she looked up, icy with affront.

'Let go of me, you big bully! I'm not deaf, I heard, and I'm here to help Annette, not make copy out of her, so leave me alone.'

She shook his hand off and he pushed it into his trouser pocket, his face grim. 'I have half a mind to make you go.'

'You and whose army?' mocked Sian furiously. 'I'm staying and there's nothing you can do about it.'

'Don't provoke me,' he said through his teeth, black-browed. 'If I choose to have you thrown out of here, you will be, don't worry, but Annette may need to have another woman around, it's true. For the present, you can stay, but take one step near a telephone and you're out.'

She gave him a seething look, but merely asked, 'Have you got any change? This machine wants coins I haven't got.' She offered him a pound coin and he pushed it aside, producing some smaller coins which he fed into the machine. Sian got her black coffee and stalked back to the waiting-room without another glance in his direction.

She sat down next to Rick, but Cass stayed outside in the corridor where she could see him pacing up and down, head bent, his hands thrust into his pockets and his face shuttered, unreadable. This must have been a hard day for him; Sian had to admit he was taking it pretty well on the whole. Few men could be trusted to behave generously after they'd had the sort of kick in the teeth which Annette had inflicted on him this morning. Sian might find him overbearing, if not downright unbearable. He might be under some delusion about his right to push people around. But he had some good qualities.

Two nurses, hurrying past with their caps a little askew and flushed faces, gave Cass a curious, grinning look, then giggled at each other. It wasn't often that they saw a man in full morning dress with a wilting buttonhole, stalking their hospital corridors like Hamlet's father on the battlements!

Cass was too absorbed in his own thoughts to notice them; his jaw showed stubble deepening and his brows were heavy with a frown. What was he thinking? Nothing cheerful, by that expression.

Rick was watching him, too, and seemed to like what he saw even less than Sian did.

'I wish he'd clear off!' he burst out suddenly, and Sian looked at him, green eyes sympathetic.

'He seems genuinely concerned about Annette's father. I think that's why he stays.'

Rick scowled, but shrugged. 'Oh, maybe. Her dad was at school with his, you know. Old Mr Cassidy died a few years back, but he and Annette's father were always good friends; they used to play chess once a week. Her dad worked for the firm when it only employed a handful of people; he worked there all his life, until he retired early. He was only fifty-six, but I think he took voluntary redundancy. He was a bit aimless once he'd stopped work. No wonder he had a heart attack when Annette ran away. He had nothing in his life but Annette, and that's Cassidy's fault. He must have asked Mr Byrne to retire early, and now he probably feels guilty.'

Sian frowned. 'I gathered that this heart condition was already known—are you sure that isn't why her father retired early?'

'Who told you that?'

'Mr Cassidy.'

Rick laughed scornfully. 'And you believed him? Annette didn't tell me that. She said they were laying a few older members of staff off, giving them a lump sum to retire early, and her father had been asked to go voluntarily. She never mentioned ill health.'

Sian screwed up the empty paper cup which had held her coffee and threw it into a waste-paper bin, where it rattled around. What was the truth? Had William Cassidy lied to her? Or had Annette been kept in the dark about her father's state of health? Sian remembered her saying that her father was worried about leaving her alone if he died—why should he have been worrying about death unless he was ill? If he was in his middle fifties that wasn't so very old, and in the natural course of events Annette should have been married with children long before her father had to face death.

'Of course,' said Rick with a faint sneer, 'it could be that Cassidy didn't want his future father-in-law working on the factory floor. He didn't really know Annette until he took her on as his secretary eighteen months ago. That was around the time her dad was asked to retire, now I remember it. Then Cassidy started showing an interest in her and dating her. He swept her off her feet—can you blame her? He could give her such a good time: flashy cars, night-spots, expensive dinners. Once he flew her to Paris in a private jet just to have lunch—showing off, dazzling her with his money. Of course she couldn't resist it. What girl could?'

'Very few,' agreed Sian drily. Nobody had ever swept her off her feet in that style; she just wished they would. It must be great to be flown to Paris in a private jet for lunch! Take me to it, she thought, grimacing.

Rick's hands balled into fists. 'So I quit,' he said. 'I wasn't staying around to watch. If she preferred him and his money, well . . .'

'But she changed her mind and ran away to you,' Sian gently reminded him.

He smiled then; his face changing. 'Yes, she came to her senses. She wouldn't have been happy with him, you know. Annette didn't grow up in that high-powered world of his, and she wasn't very easy in it. The longer it went on, the more she realised she didn't fit—with him or his friends and family.'

Sian glanced again at Cass, who was still prowling to and fro, like a tiger measuring his new captivity in a cage. Even at a distance he had a restlessly energetic air and a total assurance.

'What on earth did he see in her?' she thought aloud, then shot Rick a horrified look, but he didn't seem insulted by the question, just shrugged as though it was one he had often asked himself.

'If you want my opinion, I reckon it was a whim—she was different and he was bored. He'd have realised he had made a mistake sooner or later, but by then he might have ruined Annette's life.'

'His family didn't approve, anyway?' Sian couldn't help wondering what would have happened if Rick hadn't rung Annette on her wedding morning. Would she have gone through with the

wedding? What exactly had Rick said to her?
Hinted at suicide? Wasn't that what Annette had
said? Had Rick meant it? Or had he just been
talking wildly? Whatever he had said, it had had
quite an effect; it had broken off Annette's marriage plans, but Sian was unconvinced that Annette
knew what she was doing or what she really wanted,
even now. She was too volatile, too easily influ-
enced. She wasn't old enough to have a real relationship with a man. She ought to be by now; she
was in her early twenties, wasn't she? Sian began
to be curious about this father who lay seriously ill
up in the wards. What was he like? And how much
influence had he had on his daughter?

Rick shook his head, laughing shortly. 'You must
be joking! No, they did not approve—especially his
sister, Magdalena. She married last year, some guy
with a long pedigree, a lot of money and a face like
a Pekingese. Ever since, she's acted as if she was
too good to walk on the same ground as the rest
of us. You'd have thought that Annette was in-
sulting her by just breathing the same air. She went
out of her way to make it clear just what she
thought about the marriage.'

'Didn't you say Mr Cassidy's father was dead?'

Rick nodded. 'So is his mother—there are only
the three Cassidys left. The sister, his younger
brother Malcolm, who works in the design department, and him.' Rick jerked his head sideways
to where Cass was standing in the corridor, then
jumped to his feet as he saw that Cass was talking
to a man in a white coat.

'That could be the doctor! He looks as if he's
telling someone bad news, doesn't he? Why is he

telling Cassidy? *He* isn't marrying Annette, I am! It's me who should be talking to the doctor.' Rick headed for the door angrily, squaring his shoulders ready for battle, but before he reached them the man in the white coat began to walk in the opposite direction and Cass turned, his face grave.

Sian had followed Rick. She felt her interference might be needed if the two men came to blows.

'What's happened?' Rick demanded belligerently.

Cass looked at him with cool, grey eyes. 'His condition is still serious; it isn't hopeless, though.' He glanced sideways at Sian. 'Would you go and talk to Annette? She's very upset, it seems, but she won't leave the ward and she can't stay there. The ward sister insists that she can't see her father again tonight.'

'Of course,' Sian said, but Rick shouldered past her.

'I'll go. It's my place to be with Annette.' He glared at Cass, defying him to argue, but Cass shrugged.

'OK. Maybe you're right.'

Rick almost ran and Sian watched him, frowning. Cass watched *her*, thoughtfully. 'And what were you talking to him about? I wonder if I was wise, allowing you to come along. I keep forgetting you're a reporter. I hope you weren't milking him for information, because if you print any of this...'

'Yes?' she queried, lifting her brows at him. 'What will you do? Huff and puff and blow my house down?'

He laughed shortly. 'Something like that.'

'I'm shaking in my shoes!'

He considered her with his head slightly to one side, his mouth wry. 'I wish I was sure I could trust you.'

Green eyes alert, Sian asked, 'Oh? Why?'

'I'm faced with something of a problem. Annette can't sit up in the waiting-room all night, and they won't let her see her father even if she does, but where else is she to go? She can hardly spend the night in her own home, alone, and in the circumstances I don't think Wesley should stay there with her.'

'I don't see what this has to do with me——' Sian began, and he suddenly snapped, his face dark red with temper.

'If you let me finish, you'll understand what it has to do with you!'

'Sorry,' she said drily. He was jealous, of course; he wanted to keep Rick away from Annette, and was that surprising? He didn't want Annette to spend what should have been *their* wedding night with another man.

He ran a hand through his dark hair, mouth twisting. 'No, I'm sorry. I'm dead on my feet. This has been quite a day for me, remember.'

She nodded. 'You must be very tired.' And miserable and angry and a lot of other things, she thought, watching him with sympathy. In fact, on the whole he was behaving very well. Many men in his situation would have been quite different; bitter and vindictive, to say the least. William Cassidy was being positively saintly. Viewing the hard angles of his face, the cool assurance of those eyes, Sian suddenly wondered about that. Was his generosity entirely without motive? Surely he didn't still hope to get Annette back?

Or did he?

'I'm dying to lie down and sleep my head off,' he admitted with a self-deriding grin. 'But I can't do that until I've sorted this out. And that's where you come in. Will you stay at my house with Annette tonight?'

Sian's mouth dropped open. 'At your house?'

'If she's urgently needed at the hospital she'll have to have transport on hand and she doesn't drive. If she stays at my house I can drive her to the hospital at once, without any delay in getting a taxi.'

Sian viewed him curiously. He was certainly clever. He had made that reasoning sound very plausible, but she suspected his motives all the same.

He met her eyes, his face darkly flushed, his jaw tensed. 'Well? Will you? But if you do, I want your word that you won't print a word about all this. Just for once in your life, act like a woman, not a reporter.'

'I act like a woman most of the time,' Sian threw back, herself flushing and resenting the way he'd talked.

'Do you?' He didn't seem convinced, and his brows arched. 'Well, act like one now. Forget that Annette is in the news. She needs your help. Don't take advantage of that.'

'I ought to slap you!' Sian said, seething.

Suddenly he laughed, his face changing and a mocking amusement in his eyes. 'I wouldn't advise it. I'm bigger and tougher than you are.'

'And less scrupulous, for all your talk about my lack of scruples!' she accused him. He went on smiling down at her, but his eyes were narrowed and hard and watchful.

'Will you stay, anyway?' he asked, and she nodded, grimacing.

'I suppose so. You can have it your way.' She paused, eyeing him. 'As usual,' she added, and was furious when, instead of being angry, he grinned and looked pleased with himself.

CHAPTER THREE

'No!' Rick burst out, reddening, as soon as Cass suggested his plan. 'Annette isn't spending the night at your place. Over my dead body!'

Sian saw the look in Cass's eye and interrupted before he could retort. 'What does Annette think, though?' she coolly asked, and they all looked at Annette, who seemed quite oblivious of what was going on, her face grey and drawn. She was standing there staring at nothing, but when Sian put an arm around her Annette started violently and looked at her in shock.

'What?'

Sian gently repeated the suggestion that they should both spend the night at the Cassidy house. 'It isn't far from the hospital and if... if we had to get back here in a hurry...'

'I could drive you,' Cass said when Sian paused and looked at him.

Annette didn't even glance at him. She just nodded. 'Thank you.'

Rick frowned. 'Annette, wouldn't you rather go to a hotel or...'

'Be practical,' Cass interrupted curtly. 'At this hour no hotel would take you in. You have no luggage and you look as if you've been dragged through a hedge backwards.'

Rick glared. 'She could stay at her father's house.'

'If she needed to get back here in a hurry she would have to get a taxi, and it's much further away, too. My house is six minutes from here—her father's is at least twenty minutes away, and if she had to get a taxi that could treble the time involved.'

Annette didn't seem to be listening to their heated argument; she stood there with hanging head, hands slack at her side, body trembling slightly. Sian was worried about her. She must be exhausted; emotionally and physically drained. She looked impatiently at the two men. They were supposed to care about the girl. Why were they fighting over her instead of looking after her?

'Can we go?' she broke in sharply. 'Annette ought to be in bed.'

The men looked at Annette then, and Rick bit his lip and put his arm around her. Annette gave a sigh and leaned on him, closing her eyes. Cass turned away.

'I'll get the car and pick you up outside.'

He spun around and walked away rapidly. Sian stared after him, her brows together. Had it hurt to watch Annette cling to Rick? It must have done, of course, but William Cassidy was a strong man. He would handle his emotional scars, human beings did. Sian made a face, remembering her own pain not so long ago. It hadn't been quite as deep or as agonising as this situation must be to William Cassidy, but it had been bad for a while and she had come through it. Not that William Cassidy would thank her for telling him that, at the moment. People hated you if you said something about time healing all wounds. You couldn't blame them. Clichés were infuriating when you were hurting badly.

She almost fell asleep in the front seat of the limousine. It glided so smoothly, almost silently, through the warm night, and nobody spoke a word all the way to Cass's house.

When they pulled up at the end of a winding drive, in front of a big house whose façade she could barely see in the darkness, Rick helped Annette out and Sian stood waiting while William Cassidy unlocked the front door.

'If you want a room you're welcome to stay,' he told Rick, who reacted as if he had been stung.

'No, thanks!'

He kissed Annette, who looked up at him helplessly. 'You aren't going?'

'I'll stay with an old friend. See you tomorrow.' Rick turned and looked at Sian. 'You will take care of her?'

She nodded. 'I promise. She'll be safe while I'm around.'

Rick turned on his heel and walked away, his feet crunching on the gravelled drive, his shape soon swallowed up in the shadows of the trees lining the drive.

'I'll take you straight upstairs,' Cass said, switching on the hall light. Annette blinked and gave a stifled sigh, looking around the elegant place with hunted eyes. She had fled all this, but fate had dragged her back.

She had been here before, she knew the house, but Sian didn't, and in spite of her weariness she couldn't help feeling curious and staring around her as they followed William Cassidy upstairs.

He opened a door and gestured. 'I leave it up to you—you can either share this room, or one of you can sleep here and the other sleep in the room next door.'

Sian looked at Annette questioningly. 'What do you want to do?' The room had twin beds in it; it was spacious and beautifully furnished. She would have been quite happy sharing it with Annette, but the other girl shook her head in a tired, indifferent way.

'I'd rather be alone for a while.' She walked slowly into the room and shut the door on them. Sian frowned, and looked at Cass.

'Should we leave her alone?'

'It might be the best thing for her,' he said, frowning too, his lean face shadowed by stubble and his eyes hooded by weary lids. 'Come and see the other room.'

It was smaller, but charming: all gold and cream with brocade curtains and French period furniture, a deep-piled carpet, a bed which Sian looked at yearningly.

'I hope you'll be comfortable,' William Cassidy said, and she pulled a face at him.

'Tonight I could sleep on the floor.'

He laughed then. 'You won't have to—there's a bathroom en suite, of course, through that door, and that opens out into Annette's room, if you want to check on her during the night.' He fingered his chin, staring down at her and smiling crookedly. 'I think you may even find something to wear in the chest of drawers. This was my sister's room. She got married last year, but she didn't take all her things with her. Quite a few clothes still seem to be around. I'm pretty sure there's a nightie in one of the drawers.' He paused. 'I'd better see if Annette needs anything, too.'

'I'll do that,' Sian said quickly, and was given a slanted glance. His mouth was grim.

'Very well. Goodnight.'

The door closed with a snap. He hadn't liked it when she had insisted on dealing with Annette, she realised. Well, it had been his idea that she should come here; Rick trusted her to keep William Cassidy away from Annette, and she was going to protect the girl if she could. Annette had been through enough already today. Sian would never have acted the way Annette had; but she still felt sorry for her.

She felt a little odd, rummaging through drawers full of his sister's belongings. From what Rick had said, Magdalena Cassidy would have been indignant if she knew that a stranger, and a common reporter at that, was fingering these delicate, delicious, dreamy concoctions of satin, silk and lace, which must have cost the earth.

Surely the girl hadn't forgotten them? Or was she so wealthy that she didn't miss them and had another room full of such things in her new home? Rick had said she had married a wealthy man. Sian drew a filmy nightie out and gazed at it enviously. Lucky Magdalena. Sian could only afford nylon.

She threw the nightie over her arm and went to see if Annette was still awake. The room was in darkness and there was no sound from the bed when Sian whispered, 'Annette? Are you OK?'

Sian hesitated, though. She tiptoed over to check that Annette was actually there and saw the other girl's white face; a blur in the shadows. Annette had her eyes shut. She must have lain down fully dressed under a quilt, and she was breathing so quietly that Sian thought she might already be asleep. Well, she had had so many shocks today; she might have keeled over and fallen into a weary sleep. Sian tiptoed back to the door and returned to her own room.

She washed in the en-suite bathroom and put on Magdalena Cassidy's enchanting nightie, a floating creation of blue satin and lace by Janet Reger. She combed her hair and yawned, climbing into bed a moment later. She switched out the light and her eyes closed gratefully, only to open not long afterwards when she heard a creak on the landing outside the room.

Sian tensed, listening hard. Another creak, the rustle of someone's clothes. Was that Annette? Or was William Cassidy creeping past her room, and, if so, where was he going?

In a flash, she was out of bed and across the room. It was dark on the landing outside, but she saw a shadowy movement outside Annette's door. Sian did not want to wake the girl; she dared not make too much noise, so she hurried silently towards the shape she saw vanishing into the next room.

She caught up with him before he reached the bed, and grabbed his shoulder. He stiffened, spinning to face her.

'Outside!' Sian hissed, her eyes on the bed. Annette's face was buried in her pillow now; only her hair was visible, a drift of darkness on the white sheet.

William Cassidy hesitated, his own eyes on the bed, and Sian tugged at him, glaring.

'You shouldn't be in here,' she whispered. 'What do you think you're doing?'

At that he strode away, and she followed, softly closing the door behind her. He turned on her then, his face pale with temper.

'Who the hell do you think you are, talking to me like that in my own house?' His eyes flashed; she remembered Annette saying that he was like lightning ripping up the sky. That was how he looked now, those grey eyes violent, his tall body vibrating with a powerful tension.

'Sorry, but you asked me to look after Annette, and that's what I mean to do,' Sian said, hoping she didn't show how nervous he made her feel.

'I was making sure she was sleeping,' he said through his teeth.

'Don't you think I've checked? If she woke up and saw you by her bed she might have hysterics. She's had enough for one day, leave her alone.' She stood outside the room, her head thrown back, her eyes firmly meeting his. 'Go back to bed or do I have to sit in there all night?'

He spun on his heel and walked back past her room, and Sian followed after a pause, but as she got to her door he suddenly came back just as she was switching on her bedroom light. Startled, she faced him.

'What now?'

'You didn't really think I went in there to...' He stopped, his mouth twisting.

'Go to bed, Mr Cassidy,' said Sian, closing her door.

His foot stopped it and he shouldered through. 'You listen to me,' he said fiercely. 'As it happens, I'm too tired to rape anyone, but even if I weren't, I don't see myself hurting Annette. I'm not given to violence against women, although in your case I might be tempted.'

'Don't be,' Sian said coolly. 'Hit me and I'll hit back. You don't scare me!'

'Oh, don't I?' he said in a soft, angry voice, his mouth a white line.

'No, you don't,' Sian said with more assurance than she felt, trying to stare him down.

He slowly ran his eyes over her, from her ruffled blonde hair, down over the curve of her slim body in the clinging blue satin, to the pale, bare feet showing beneath the deep lace hem. Until then, Sian hadn't been self-conscious, but she began to feel heat flowing under her skin, and her body trembled. Aghast, she swallowed; what was wrong with her?

He was doing it deliberately, of course; his flickering gaze was intended to make her wildly conscious of being half-naked and alone with him at night, and it succeeded. Sian read the intention, the mockery, but she saw something else in those grey eyes: a real sensuality that made her go weak at the knees. Worse than that, she felt an answering emotion. She was attracted to him; it was pure chemistry she felt leaping between them, like a white flame. It made no sense; they had only just met and didn't know each other, he had just been going to marry another girl, and she was in no hurry to get involved with another man after her last emotional crash.

She knew what was behind William Cassidy's mood, too. He was in turmoil over Annette; jealous, hurt, bitter, he had gone into that room . . . to do what? Sian looked into his eyes and wondered. He had just said he was too tired to rape anyone; but what had been in his mind? What was in it now?

'Go to bed, Mr Cassidy,' she repeated, her voice icing over. 'This has been a bad day for you and I'm very sorry, but don't take it out on me. I'm not to blame. You say you're tired and I believe you. I'm tired, too. If I don't get some sleep soon I'll go out of my mind, so can we please stop playing stupid games?'

For a moment, he just stared at her fixedly, then the strange, harsh light dissolved in his eyes and he gave a twisted smile, and yawned.

'Cool, aren't you? And right, of course. Goodnight.'

He went so suddenly that it was another moment before Sian realised she was alone. She closed her door, then, listening to the soft departing footsteps until the house was silent again, she stumbled back to bed and lay down. Sleep didn't just come—it fell on her like a house, smothering her.

When she woke up it was morning; light filled the room and she lay in a state of confusion for a while until she remembered where she was and what had happened the night before. She slid out of bed in a hurry and ran at once to the next room. Annette still slept heavily, her breathing regular. Sian crept out again and came face to face with William Cassidy once more.

He was fully dressed, but differently. This morning he wore a black polo-neck sweater over a cream silk shirt and casual grey trousers. Sian wondered if he had slept at all. He had shaved, clearly; his skin was smooth and faintly damp, and so was his dark hair, as if he had recently showered.

'Good morning,' he said. 'Is Annette awake?'

She shook her head. 'She's dead to the world. Any news from the hospital?'

'Her father made it through the night, if that's what you mean, but it's still touch and go. He's not conscious, though, so there's no real point in her going there until later. Let her sleep while she can.'

'Did you?' asked Sian curiously, turning towards her own room.

'For a few hours. You?'

Sian wished he would stop looking her over like that; it made her self-conscious and it was annoying because it must be automatic—the man was hooked on Annette. She wouldn't be surprised if he had already been in there this morning, checking on her.

'My housekeeper will have breakfast on the table in fifteen minutes,' he said as she closed the door of her room. 'If you're hungry, that is.'

'I'll be down,' Sian said, making for the bathroom to shower.

It was almost eight-thirty by her watch when she made her way downstairs, after checking again on Annette. Sian paused in the white-panelled hall, her gaze flying around it curiously. She hadn't had a chance to orientate herself in the house last night when they had arrived, and hadn't a clue where to go from here, but she admired the look of the place—flowers everywhere, the deep gleam of highly polished wood, a long-case clock near the foot of the stairs, a silver carriage clock on a table, reflected in an Art Nouveau mirror in a painted wood frame. The effect was charming. Was William Cassidy's housekeeper responsible for the well-cared-for look? She hadn't been in evidence last night, and Sian wondered where she was this morning. Maybe she was one of those invisible servants people had in fairy-tales. I wish I had one too, Sian thought, smiling.

'What's funny?'

His deep voice made her jump. She hadn't noticed him walking up behind her, and she spun around to face him, eyes wide and very bright.

'Oh, hello! I was wondering where to go.'

'I thought we'd eat in the morning-room,' he said, and she laughed.

'Oh, by all means!' she said drily, getting a hard, unamused look from him.

'I'd better check on Annette first, though.'

'I just did,' Sian said, stepping in front of him as he made for the stairs.

Their eyes met; his narrowed and hers were very green and very ironic.

'You've got the wrong impression,' he muttered. 'You don't need to protect Annette from me. I wouldn't harm a hair on her head.'

'I'm sorry, but you scare her,' Sian said, and his eyes blazed.

'I do what?' His voice rose, and there was violence in it.

Sian grimaced. 'If you snarl at her like that, I'm
not surprised she gets scared!'

'I wasn't snarling,' he snarled.

Sian laughed and saw his angry eyes blink. He
looked hard at her and ran a hand through that
thick, dark hair.

'I'm starving. Can we eat?' Sian looked around.
'Where is this morning-room?'

He gestured. 'This way.' They walked down a
narrow corridor and into a sunny, square room
overlooking a rose-garden. Sian went to the window
and stared out, glad of the sunlight on her face,
inhaling the dewy morning scent of the roses. She
couldn't see any other building; the garden was
enormous and bordered on one side by a high red-
brick wall; on the other by the dark, secret mass
of the New Forest. The garden was as immaculate
as the house; the lawns smooth-shaven and edged
with flowerbeds bursting with colour. He must keep
quite a large staff, but they were not in evidence.

'What a lovely garden,' she said, turning back
into the room.

'Thank you.' He held a chair back for her. 'Come
and eat.'

As she sat down, a woman in a white apron
bustled into the room carrying a tray of food which
she began setting down on the table. Sian watched
curiously, met the woman's brown eyes, and got a
quick, friendly smile.

'Good morning,' she said.

'Good morning, miss,' replied the housekeeper. 'I've made some scrambled eggs and bacon, but if there's anything else you'd like...'

'That sounds marvellous, thank you.'

The woman put out a rack of toast, freshly made and golden brown, ran a glance over the table and left. Sian poured herself some freshly squeezed orange juice and helped herself to some egg and a piece of toast. There was a pile of Sunday newspapers at William Cassidy's elbow. He nodded to them and asked, 'Want one of these?'

'Please,' she said. 'My own paper first.' It was a pity she had to remind him, but she wanted to see the story in print; find out what the subs had done to her copy. She watched the frown appear on that lean face, the eyes glitter and the mouth harden, but he flicked over the papers and threw her own over to her without commenting.

They ate their breakfast in silence. Sian wryly noted the changes that had been made in the story and wondered how William Cassidy would react when he read it. He wasn't going to like it. But then, nobody ever did like what you said about them; she had learnt that long ago. In cold print a fact would look like an accusation; a comment could become painful. She had reported what Annette had said to her and she hadn't invented a word, but would William Cassidy believe that?

She put the paper down, and poured herself some more coffee, then glanced enquiringly at him. 'Can I refill your cup?'

'Thanks.' He held it out, looking at the paper by her plate. 'Finished with that?'

She reluctantly handed it to him, wishing she hadn't been around when he saw it. Sipping her coffee, she took another paper and glanced through that. They had the story, of course, but not in the same detail, or from the inside, as she had.

Sian would have felt triumph at that; it was always fun to get an exclusive, to scoop the others, but at present she was more interested in William Cassidy's reaction. She heard a rustle as his long fingers tightened on the pages, the thick sound of his angry breathing, and bit her lip in apprehension. She hoped he wasn't going to turn violent.

He suddenly flung the paper across the table, knocking over the jug of orange juice. 'I ought to wring your neck!' he grated.

Sian snatched up her linen table-napkin and hurriedly began to mop at the spreading orange stain, glad to have something to do. 'I realise it can't have been pleasant to read,' she said, and he made a furious noise.

'You've made me sound like some sort of ogre.'

'I just wrote what Annette had said.' Sian came out with that before she had thought about it, and wished she hadn't because it wasn't the most tactful excuse, was it?

His face darkened with angry blood. 'Annette's known me most of her life—ever since she was a toddler, in fact. It's true we didn't know each other all that well until she started working for me in my office, but for heaven's sake, she was going to marry me. Even if she changed her mind, she can't have hated me enough to talk about me as if I . . . and to a total stranger, too!'

She watched him with anxious sympathy; she felt guilty. She had never had to face anyone she had written about in that intimate way. It put her job into a new perspective for her. She had hurt this man! She bit her lower lip, watching him uneasily.

Her career had been ultra-important to her until that moment; she had never questioned its validity or hesitated to sacrifice anything in the pursuit of it. This was a first for her.

'You probably invented most of this!' he accused her, but she didn't deny it angrily. She stayed silent, her lashes lowered, her green eyes watching him through them. He stayed silent too, staring back. Suddenly she saw his mouth twitch, his body slacken from the tense rage that had held it.

'Stop looking at me like that!' he said softly, in a very different tone, and Sian lifted her lashes, and widened her eyes at him in query.

'How was I looking at you?'

His stare held an amused intimacy that made her heart skip a beat in surprise. '*You* are a very annoying woman,' he drawled, and at that moment Annette ran into the room, breathless and white-faced.

'Is there any news? Is my father...why didn't you wake me?'

Cass was on his feet at once and beside her, putting an arm round her. Annette didn't shrink away, as Sian half expected; she leaned on him, looking up into his face imploringly.

'I've talked to the hospital. He's a little better this morning. When you've had some breakfast we'll go back there.'

'I couldn't eat! I want to go now.'

'No, Annette. At least drink some tea and have some toast! It won't take two minutes, but if you don't eat you might be ill, and that won't help your father, will it?' Cass used a gentle, reasoning voice, the voice one might use to a child, and Annette sighed, her face helpless.

'Come and sit down,' Cass said, leading her to the table.

Annette looked at Sian as she sat down opposite her, in the seat next to where Cass had been sitting. For a moment Sian felt the other girl didn't remember her; Annette frowned, stared, then said, 'Oh, hello!'

'Hello, Annette.' Sian poured her some tea while Cass vanished in search of fresh toast.

Annette drank the tea without appearing to be aware what she was doing.

'Where did Ricky go?'

She was in shock, Sian realised at that instant. Her eyes held a dazed blankness that was rather worrying.

'To stay with a friend. He'll probably see you at the hospital.'

Annette was on her feet again. 'We must go!'

Cass came back before she reached the door, and stopped her. 'The toast is on its way, and I rang the hospital again. You couldn't see him even if you went now, because he's fast asleep.'

Annette sagged again and let him put her back on the chair, her slim body like that of a rag doll. Sian watched Cass's gentleness and a funny little ache started inside her. Considering the humiliation Annette had inflicted on him yesterday, he was amazingly kind to her and that must mean that he loved Annette very much. There was no rational explanation why that should bother Sian; she didn't really know either of them very well, yet that ache went on inside her and all her cool self-derision couldn't stop it.

The housekeeper brought the toast on a plate and looked at Annette in a muddled way—half sympathy, half resentment—before stamping out again. Annette didn't notice; she was past noticing anything. Sian put toast on her plate and offered her marmalade or honey.

Annette shook her head, ate the buttered toast with reluctance, as if it were sawdust, but at least had drunk her tea, into which Sian had stirred a heavy dose of sugar. Annette didn't appear to notice that, either.

She had almost finished her toast when a new arrival made them all start. They heard the bang of the front door, footsteps in the hall, then there was a whirl of skirts and a very beautiful girl hurtled into the room, her arms full of newspapers.

'Cass, I could kill her!' she began before she saw them all. Then she stared, her jaw dropping, her lips parted on a gasp of furious incredulity.

She looked vaguely like her brother. Sian saw the family likeness—the black hair and pale eyes, the height, the pared bone structure and finely moulded features. Sian had never seen a photo of Magdalena, yet she felt at once that this was his sister.

'We'd better talk in the hall, Magda,' Cass said, confirming this, getting up and moving towards his sister.

'What's *she* doing here?' his sister demanded, flushing to her hairline, as she stared at Annette. Sian admired the white dress she wore; it was very simple, very chic. Magdalena's expression was in direct contrast; it was complicated and well-nigh barbaric. She was in a tearing temper, and scowled at Annette, who didn't seem aware that she was there at all, and went on drinking her tea with a blank expression.

'Out,' Cass said, taking his sister's arm, but she resisted him and stood her ground, glaring and getting angrier by the second.

'How can you bear to have her in the same room after what she did to you? My God, when I think about it! I didn't know where to look. I was so embarrassed, and last night people kept ringing up to sympathise...that's a joke! What they really wanted to do was winkle all the details out of me, have a good laugh! She humiliated us, not just you, Cass—the whole family! Have you read these papers? All the money you spend on public relations, I'd have thought they could keep this out of the gutter press. What do you pay them for?' She took a deep breath, but she hadn't finished. 'What's she doing here, anyway? One of the papers said she'd run off to some man in London, stood you up for one of your own staff! So why is she back? You can't be fool enough to consider giving her another chance? I won't let you. I...'

'Shut up,' Cass snarled, and her eyes rounded in shock.

He gripped her elbow and hustled her out of the room. Sian heard their voices rising and falling in the hall. Annette had finished her breakfast; she looked at her watch and made a husky little noise, a half-sob.

'Can't we go?'

The front door banged violently; the angry voices no longer snapped at each other.

'In a minute,' soothed Sian, watching the door of the room.

Cass came through it, frowning heavily, his skin dark with angry colour, his eyes glittering.

'Cass, we must go,' Annette pleaded, getting up, and he looked at her blankly for a second, then smiled reassurance.

'Yes, I'll get the car. Wait for me outside.'

Sian followed him into the hall, and he looked down at her impatiently as she caught up with him. 'Well, what now?'

'Look, I can't stay here much longer, you know. I do have my own life to lead. I've got to be back at work tomorrow, so I'll have to be back in London tonight.'

'Can't you take a few days off?' He ran a hand through his smoothly brushed hair until it all stood on end to match his distracted, irritated expression.

'I just did. I'm not entitled to any more.'

'Ring your paper and ask...'

'Ask my editor if I can stay?' Sian laughed shortly. 'Oh, he would say yes. He'd jump at it! He would also expect a follow-up to my first scoop—the latest inside dope on Annette's flight from the altar.'

Her dry tone made him scowl, staring. 'You could refuse to write it, couldn't you? If you really like Annette, you won't put her through any more.'

'Let me remind you, from tomorrow I am due back at work. If I stay I shall technically be working.'

His mouth indented. 'Oh, very well. I'll make other arrangements for Annette, but can you hang on for a few hours to give me a chance to work something out?'

She felt small and mean under his accusing eyes but, however much he disapproved of her, she couldn't bear to stay here. She had to get away, from him and from having to watch him with Annette. Was his sister right? Did he hope to get Annette back? It was none of Sian's business, but she couldn't believe those two were suited. Annette was right out of his league—couldn't he see that? Annette herself had realised it, even if only at the last minute. Or had she always known it, but only found the courage to run away at the eleventh hour? Even then she probably wouldn't have gone if Rick hadn't rung her and galvanised her into flight.

'OK,' she said flatly, staring at him and bewildered by his blindness about Annette. They would have been a very ill-matched couple—why couldn't he see that?

He turned and walked out of the house and she stared after him, that queer little pain nagging away inside her again. I'm jealous, she thought, wide-eyed with shock. How stupid! I'm jealous—but I hardly know the man, so why should I be?

She might not know him well, but one thing she was sure about it—she'd be more on his level than Annette had ever been.

Hot colour ran up to her hair. How ridiculous, she thought, angry with herself. What on earth made me think that? He wouldn't give me a second look!

Oh, but he has, her mind reminded her; he's looked more than twice, in fact. She stared at nothing, remembering the times when she had felt that powerful flare of attraction—or had she imagined it? Had she wanted to believe he was as aware of her as she was of him? It was so easy to deceive yourself—wasn't that what Cass was doing over Annette? If he thought they could ever be happy together he was deceiving himself. If Sian hadn't heard Annette's side of it already she would have been just as sure that marriage between Cass and Annette would be a recipe for disaster. The two of them were worlds apart. Why couldn't he see that?

'Are we going yet?' Annette said huskily behind her, and Sian turned and hurriedly smiled reassurance.

'Let's wait outside the house.'

Cass drew up shortly after that, and they drove to the hospital to find it besieged by reporters and photographers who jostled each other to get pictures of them arriving.

Cass and Sian hurried Annette into the hospital, and the burly porters held the clamouring mob back while they escaped up to the heart unit. Annette was in tears by then; Cass had his arm around her and was murmuring gently, but his grey eyes acidly reminded Sian that the mob outside were her people, she was one of them. Sian looked away, wishing she could deny it. This was one of those times when silence was the only defence.

They found Rick in the waiting-room. He came to take Annette away from Cass, his face jealous, resentful. Annette cried harder at the sight of him and clung, her arms round his neck.

'Oh, Rick, he isn't worse? Why can't I see him? I'm so scared. He isn't going to die, is he? Outside there are... they all shouted and tried to grab me as if I was a criminal or something... what's going on? When can I see my father?'

Rick had both arms round her, his chin on her soft hair. 'The sister says you can take a look at him, but he's under sedation, he won't know you're there. He's OK, though, Annette. He's going to be OK, in time. Whatever happens, you mustn't upset yourself or he may pick it up. You've got to be very calm and quiet before you see him.'

She struggled with her tears, shaking. 'I am, Rick. I'm calm and quiet.'

'Come and see Sister,' said Rick, leading her out, ignoring Sian and Cass. Sian sat down, grimacing, avoiding Cass's eye. Did it wound him to see Annette with Rick, to be forced to relinquish her to the other man? She wished she could leave at once, get away from here.

Cass prowled up and down, his hands in his pockets, his head bent, his face dark. Rick came back and Cass looked sharply at him.

'She's in there with her father.' Rick had a hospital mask tied round his neck, and had obviously just pushed it down from his mouth. He faced Cass belligerently. 'There's no need for you to stay. She doesn't want you here; I can take care of her from now on. Tonight, I'll take her to stay with my aunt.

I've got a car, so that I can drive her back here in an emergency.'

Cass listened, his face a mask. He didn't answer, just nodded, and Rick turned on his heel and went, pulling up the mask over his mouth again. Cass stared after him and then turned to look at Sian.

'I'll drive you back to London now,' was all he said, in a quiet voice, but Sian would have given a great deal to know exactly what he was feeling.

CHAPTER FOUR

CASS didn't talk much on the drive back to London, and Sian was relieved about that because her thoughts were chaotic, and she needed to be quiet to sort them out into some sort of order. So much had happened in far too short a time, both around her, and inside her. She was bewildered, dazed, unsure—in fact, the only thing she was sure about at the moment was that she wasn't sure precisely how she *did* feel.

And he was the cause: this frowning man sitting beside her! He had done this to her! She looked sideways, through her lashes, and watched him driving, his grey eyes hard and fixed, his profile unyielding. A queer little tremor ran through her; an electric shock along her nerves.

It was crazy. She barely knew the man. It wasn't even twenty-four hours since he had first walked into her life, why should he have this devastating effect on her? Am I that impressionable? she asked herself, closing her eyes to shut out all sight of that lean, dark face in profile, the wind-blown hair giving him the look of some marauding barbarian, a dangerous invader coming unstoppably towards you while you stared, paralysed.

My imagination has run mad, she thought, laughter in her throat as she realised what she had been thinking. At that moment, Cass turned his head, still dark-browed, and snapped, 'What's funny?'

'I am,' she said, and he stopped scowling and looked surprised.

'Why?'

'Never mind, something I was thinking.' She looked at the speedometer and winced. 'Do we have to drive at this speed?' The car was touching ninety although it ran so smoothly that she hadn't realised it until then.

'Yes,' he said coolly.

'Soothes the savage breast, does it?'

Her mockery made him laugh. 'Something like that.'

'It may be doing you a power of good, but it makes me feel sick,' Sian said frankly, and he grimaced.

'Sorry about that. I was miles away.'

Sian could guess where, but carefully said nothing. He took his foot off the accelerator, and the speed began to fall. Sian gave a faint sigh of relief and he grinned wryly at her.

'That's better, is it?'

'Sixty-five is bearable,' she said, leaning back in her seat and relaxing.

'We're only half an hour from London,' he told her a moment later. 'In time for lunch—will you let me give you lunch? I owe you a lunch at least, wouldn't you say?'

'That's OK,' she said, meaning that he didn't owe her anything and there was no need to buy her lunch, but he misunderstood, either deliberately or because he really didn't get what she meant.

'Fine, why don't we eat at a pretty little riverside pub I know? It's a lovely day and the landlord is a friend of mine. The place will be packed out, but he keeps a couple of tables in his garden for friends on fine days. It's quite an experience—Danny was a jazz musician—he can play anything you care to name—and while he was travelling up and down the country doing gigs he taught himself to cook like an angel. You won't get better food in London.'

'What's the pub called?' she asked, wondering how he had met a jazz musician who cooked like an angel. Of course, there was no point in being curious about him or his life because after today they weren't going to be meeting.

He talked about the pub for several minutes, then asked her, 'How long have you been in journalism?'

Sian realised he was only making polite conversation, but she answered him because anything was better than sitting next to him, brooding over the weird effect he had on her, or sensing him brooding over Annette. At least he wasn't doing that while he chatted about jazz and Fleet Street.

'Ever since I left school and joined the local newspaper,' she told him.

'You've done well to get this far!' he commented, eyeing her speculatively. 'You must be good or you wouldn't be working in Fleet Street at your age. You can't be much more than twenty-three or four.'

She laughed. 'How flattering! Try twenty-five.' Almost twenty-six, actually, she thought, but why be utterly frank with him? Somehow twenty-five didn't sound as old as twenty-six, although she couldn't quite say why.

He shrugged. 'That's still pretty young.' He grinned suddenly at her. 'I speak from experience. I can give you ten years.'

She had guessed his age, but he looked younger at times. He was very fit, very lean; his body had the suppleness of a much younger man. She secretly assessed him, her eyes flicking down over him, then up again. As her gaze reached his face, she found him watching her, his mouth crooked with amusement. Sian went red and looked away, burning with embarrassment.

'Well?' he murmured teasingly.

'Well what?' She was furious because, for all her efforts to sound cool, she knew her voice was husky.

'Do I pass?'

She hesitated, torn between rage and laughter, then gave in and laughed. 'Oh, you'd do, on a dark night,' she said, and he laughed too, his head thrown back and his laughter open and full of enjoyment.

Sian was still very hot, and stared out of the window at the grey mass of London's huddled streets as they drove towards the centre, off the motorway. Then Cass turned towards the river to follow it along its curving path, through sprawling suburbs, until they reached the riverside pub, a whitewashed Georgian building set in a garden of lawns and flowerbeds, with willows edging the riverbank just below it.

Cass was right; it was packed with people that Sunday lunch time, and there were cars parked like sardines in the large car park adjoining it, but the landlord welcomed Cass with a wide grin and friendly eyes which held an unspoken sympathy.

He must have read about the wedding fiasco, but he didn't breathe a word about it.

'A table in the garden? Of course, I'll get Nell to lay it right away. There isn't anyone else out there, today; you'll have the garden to yourself. But come and have a drink with me in my office first. It's ages since we saw you here.'

'I've been busy, I'm afraid,' Cass said, following him into a tiny room, just big enough for a desk covered with papers and a couple of filing-cabinets. Cass sat down on the window-seat which was piled with red velvet cushions, and patted the place next to him, gesturing for Sian to sit there.

The landlord asked what they would drink and poured them glasses, handing them over with a smile as he saw Sian staring at the four walls which were crowded with sketches in pen and pencil: some quite lovely landscapes, others funny and often savage cartoons.

'Didn't Cass tell you I drew?'

'You did them all?'

Her stupefaction made him laugh, brushing his long brown hair back from his thin face.

'All of them, I'm afraid. Whenever I get five minutes to myself, I open my sketchpad.'

'Cass only told me you cooked!'

Danny roared. 'Isn't that typical? He's a materialist, our Cass—just interested in the body, not the soul. Isn't that so, Cass?'

'Let's say the pleasures of the body are easier to get hold of!'

Sian laughed, then met his eyes and flushed, the mockery in his glance reminding her of her own covert assessment of him in the car not long ago.

'But isn't jazz soul music?' Cass asked Danny lightly. 'You know I love jazz. Doesn't that qualify?'

'OK, I take it back—you do have some unmaterialistic tendencies,' Danny agreed, grinning. 'But not many. Nobody who has made as much money as you have can be anything but materialistic.'

'What's wrong with a little ambition? Sian, you're ambitious, aren't you?'

'To be a good journalist, yes,' she agreed.

'To be a success,' Cass insisted, and she had to admit he was right.

'Just as Danny once dreamt of being a great jazzman,' Cass drawled, grinning, and Danny made a face at him.

'You wouldn't have minded that yourself!' he teased, and Cass laughed.

'Really? You wanted to play jazz?' asked Sian, eyes widening in disbelief.

'He certainly did, once upon a time, before the business bug hit him,' Danny told her, an eye on Cass, who was looking wryly amused.

'What did you play?' asked Sian. Then grinning, she added, 'Don't tell me—your own trumpet!'

Danny roared and Cass pretended to punch her. 'Very funny, but it was clarinet, actually, and a little bit of sax.'

'Did you say sex?' asked Danny innocently, and Cass pulled a face at him.

'She knows I meant saxophone, so don't try that old chestnut on her, or I won't send a man down to mend your computer next time it breaks down.'

'Talking about that . . .' Danny began, and Cass interrupted quickly.

'Not on your life! I'm not looking at it now. I'm hungry and it's Sunday and I want my lunch.' He finished his drink and stood up. 'Come on, Sian, let's get out into the garden before he drags me off to his den.'

The garden was lovely: a small, isolated part of the public gardens, walled off and secret, with rambling roses spilling torrents of red and gold flowers down the walls, lavender scenting the air, a sycamore giving shade and a table and chairs placed on a little patio for them to eat under a yellow umbrella.

'How long have you known Danny?' Sian asked at one point, and Cass shrugged.

'Years now. I was twenty, so was he. He was playing jazz up at Cambridge while I was in college there; he was a student too that year, but he got sent down because he never did a stroke of work. Just made music in the local pubs and clubs. I thought his was a great life for a while. I sat in on some of their sessions in my spare time but, unlike Danny, I did work. My family expected it, and I didn't have either the courage or the motivation to take Danny's route. So I stayed and went into business, and Danny dropped out. He did OK. He's got this place and a lot of friends. He still plays jazz when he feels like it, and we've always kept in touch. He's a nice guy.'

Sian nodded, agreeing, but as she watched the river flowing under the slanting green willows, she thought that Cass was quite a nice guy, too, and full of surprises. She would never have suspected him of wanting to be a jazz musician.

'Why electronics?' she asked him idly, and he answered the same way, in between eating the duck which was their second course.

'Who knows why? As Danny says, I got the bug. Computers came along while I was still young enough to get obsessed with them the way Danny was about jazz. I'm one of those lucky people, in fact, whose hobby is their way of earning a living.' He smiled at her across the table, sunlight turning his grey eyes silver. 'Like yourself!'

Her heart gave a funny little sideways kick and she flushed, as if he might be able to tell what his smile had done to her heartbeat. Her eyes fled and hunted across the garden, but she felt Cass watching her—but thinking what?

'You were right, this food is marvellous,' she said huskily, although she hadn't really thought about what she was eating and couldn't quite remember the first course. Had it been a tossed salad with croûtons and hot cheese? Or hadn't it? She hadn't tasted a thing or looked properly. She had been looking at Cass and watching dappled sunlight playing over his face and hair.

'Isn't it?' he drawled, but something in his voice made her doubly self-conscious. She didn't dare look at him again.

When they had drunk their excellent coffee, they went for a stroll along the river under the willows. The afternoon was hot, and there were lots of other people out, some walking, others rowing a boat on the water with the ducks scattering around them, squawking and demanding bread.

They sat down on the grass under a shady tree and talked for a while, but Sian tried not to catch his eye or let the conversation touch on anything personal or intimate. She kept their talk firmly centred on books, films, television, current affairs, and skimmed over the surface even then. She did not want to get too close to him or let him get too close.

Perhaps she had known on sight, or perhaps the realisation had grown on her gradually—but she was now quite convinced that this man could hurt her, and she wasn't going to let that happen.

They went back to the pub and chatted to Danny for a while, then said goodbye and drove back into London. Sian firmly intended to say goodbye to Cass in the car. She did not want him in her flat; partly because that would be like letting him into her life, the really private core of her life. She might see him in the rooms when he wasn't there, just as when she leaned back in the car and closed her eyes she still saw his dark, lean face glimmering on the inside of her lids.

He could easily become an obsession. Sian didn't want that. When they drew up outside the building, she hurriedly began to gabble a thank you, her hand on the door-handle.

'Wonderful meal, lovely place to spend a Sunday, thank you very much and I hope Annette's father gets over his heart attack and everything is OK.' She took a deep breath. 'Well, thank you, goodbye.'

She didn't dare look at him. She swung her legs out and quickly slammed the car door behind her, almost running across the pavement. She heard his voice behind her and ran faster, until the sound was too far away to hear. She didn't stop running until she was inside her flat with the door firmly closed; then she leaned on the door, breathing hard and torn between relief and a funny seeping feeling of depression.

She would never see him again. She was glad about that. She never wanted to see him again; she could do very well without a man in her life at the moment. Men were too much trouble: they wanted too much of you, they demanded more than just your attention now and then, they resented everything else in your life if it came between you and them. Louis had been violent about it!

It must be their mothers, Sian decided, straightening with a sigh. Mothers encouraged their sons to think the world revolved around them.

The doorbell rang loudly and she jumped about six feet in the air, staring at the door with round eyes and an open mouth.

The bell rang again, even more loudly. Sian reluctantly opened the door and Cass stood there.

'Look——' she began aggressively, then stopped as he held out her handbag.

'You were in such a hurry that you left this in the car.'

She groaned. 'Oh, thanks. Sorry.'

'So why?' he asked, ominously advancing.

'Why what?' Sian tried to block his way without being too obvious about it.

'Why the hurry?' He sauntered round her, as if unaware that she was trying to keep him out, and she didn't like to be rude or ask him to go. Flustered, she looked up at him and then wished she hadn't, because his grey eyes were amused, and looking up reminded her how tall he was and how much she was attracted to him.

'Oh,' she said, confused. 'The hurry? Yes, well, I have a lot to do.'

His dark brows rose in incredulous arches. 'At this hour?'

'I start work again tomorrow, after my holiday,' she said huskily, her throat hot.

His expression changed, darkened. 'You weren't planning on writing any more stories about me and Annette, I hope? I thought we had an agreement about that.'

Sian blinked; nothing had been further from her mind than Annette or the office, yet under his stare she became guilty, her colour rising.

'You were!' Cass concluded, black-browed, eyes glittering. 'I must have been crazy to think I could trust a reporter! You've been playing some devious little game, have you? Lulling my suspicions, getting me to talk about myself. I was stupid enough to fall for it, too! God knows what I've been telling you.'

As he bit out the angry sentences he advanced on her and Sian backed away, her dazed eyes wide with alarm. She was too stunned to argue or deny it, she just shook her head helplessly, like a fool, until she found herself in the sitting-room; tripping over the leg of a chair she didn't see until too late.

She gave a muffled cry and instinctively clutched at the nearest stable object, which turned out to be Cass, who promptly caught her before she fell headlong, but looked at her with such rage that she wished she had grabbed at something else.

'I've a good mind to...' he began thickly, staring down at her, then his eyes moved downwards to fix on her startled, parted lips.

He was silent, staring. Sian breathed roughly, trembling, watching him and hanging on to him with both hands because she was still off balance, and if he let go of her she would tumble to the floor. She tried to say something, but not a sound came out before Cass slowly lowered his head towards her.

Sian's thoughts were a battleground. Common sense told her to stop him, push him away, before this went any further, but the irrational, emotional side of her had other ideas, had been having them ever since she met William Cassidy. She had been attracted from that first look, and she was dying to know how it felt to kiss him, to be kissed.

Curiosity killed the cat. She closed her eyes and her mouth parted to meet his. In the warm, smothering darkness of the kiss she forgot everything else for a while; her head spun and her body seemed boneless. How was it possible to stand on your own two feet and stay upright when your flesh was melting and on fire? She clung to him weakly and felt his hands moving: sliding and stroking along her back, holding her closer, caressing her, a sensual, intimate exploration which echoed what she wanted, what she was doing to him—touching his neck, his back, his powerful chest.

He was breathing faster, and he was very hot; his skin burned her fingers and alarm bells rang in her head.

What am I doing? she thought, suddenly disturbed, taking fright. They were moving too fast. This was crazy!

Every man she had ever got mixed up with had hurt her, led her into trouble. They always wanted more than she was ready to give—they were never satisfied with part of her; they wanted to swallow her up. They resented everything else in her life—her career, her friendships, her family. In fact, they were jealous of anything that took her away from them even for a few hours. They were like babies demanding to be the centre of the universe.

Sian had made a decision after her split with Louis—no more men for at least a year! She didn't want a love-life until her love and her life were one; until she met someone who could love her without wanting to own her, someone who left her space in which to be herself, room to be free. The trouble was, the world wasn't over-populated with men like that! They were a special breed, and William Cassidy almost certainly didn't belong to it. Sian had a suspicion he was very much of the breed she most resented—the old-style, demanding male with the macho self-image and the ego to match.

She had seen how he tried to take over Annette's life—and presumably he loved Annette, or why else should he have wanted to marry her?

Sian felt a sick qualm deep inside her. Why was she letting him make love to her when she knew he would prefer to be holding another woman? She had let her own instincts drive her—when would she learn that that was folly? Her head should rule her, not her body nor her heart. If she had let it do that a few moments ago she wouldn't feel this bitter humiliation, this distaste.

Wrenching herself backwards, she said sharply, 'No, I won't be used as some sort of consolation prize because Annette walked out on you!'

Cass looked dazed for a second or two, staring down at her in blank silence, then his flush became a dark tide of colour running to his hairline, and his grey eyes iced over.

'I wasn't...' he began, and she interrupted in a snarl.

'Oh, yes, you were! Yesterday you were all set to marry Annette—so don't tell me you wanted me for myself, because I wouldn't believe you. You're angry and upset and I'm sorry—but I'm not handing myself over to make you feel better.'

His hands gripped her shoulders, he shook her angrily, glaring. 'For heaven's sake, all I did was kiss you!'

'It was turning into something else very fast!' Sian muttered, pushing his hands away. 'And let go! You're hurting me and I won't be manhandled.'

'A minute ago you seemed to like the way I was touching you,' he said in a voice she hated.

She was scarlet and tense from head to foot. 'Get out of my flat!' she hissed at him, her hands curling into claws at her side.

'Sure you really want me to go?' he drawled in that soft, cold, taunting voice, and Sian snarled back.

'I'm certain!'

'But are you?' he mocked without budging an inch, and she grew increasingly nervous, because he was bigger and stronger than she was, and if he refused to go how could she make him?

'Go away,' she snapped, and he laughed, but his eyes weren't amused. They scared her because they told her just how angry he was—not a red-hot anger, but a frozen one, which was far worse.

'You just reminded me that you're not Annette,' he said, coming closer. 'But all women are the same under the skin—they love to play little games, use their claws, tease and torment. That's why you let me kiss you just now, isn't it? You wanted to find out what turned me on, what power you could have over me. There's nothing like sex to give away what makes a man tick, but you weren't prepared to go that far. You just played a little game and then backed off.'

Sian's mouth was dry with fear at that soft, cold, frightening voice. She looked into his eyes and swallowed. She had never seen a man this angry before, and hurried to placate him, her voice husky.

'No, you're wrong. I wasn't playing games...'

'What were you doing, then?' he asked, smiling, and she wished he wouldn't keep smiling, because it made the anger in his eyes so much worse.

'I...' She felt as if her mouth was full of ashes; her lips were parched, and she moistened them with her tongue, hunting for something to say to soothe him.

'Someone ought to teach you a lesson,' he said, and her body was at once rigid with icy panic.

'Don't you touch me,' she whispered, unable to take her eyes off him, staring into his eyes like a hypnotised rabbit in front of a snake poised for the kill.

'Didn't it ever occur to you that one day some man might turn nasty? That one of your little games might backfire?' He slowly looked her up and down in a way she found quite terrifying. Shuddering, Sian wanted to cry, and almost did, but didn't because rage began to grow inside her, the anger of someone pushed to the limit by fear. She stiffened her spine and lifted her head, glaring back at him.

'Don't try to make me pay for what Annette did to you!' His set gaze flickered and he frowned, but she didn't give him a chance to answer. She raised her voice and almost shouted, 'That wasn't my fault, Mr Cassidy. In fact, it wasn't anybody's fault, not even yours, nor Annette's. It should be obvious to you that if your marriage had gone through it would have been the most monumental mistake and you'd regret it. Annette didn't love you. She should never have said she'd marry you, and I'm not making excuses for her, but she's not too bright where running her own life is concerned. Frankly, I think you were lucky, because Annette is a helpless sort of girl and you don't strike me as the type to enjoy having a wife who's always crying and wringing her hands, but maybe I'm wrong. Maybe that's just the sort of woman you fancy. I don't know and I don't care, but you aren't punishing me for any of that.'

'I wasn't,' he said, and the ice had gone; his eyes were no longer set in that frozen wasteland, but Sian was still wary of him.

'You just said some pretty nasty things to me, and don't try to kid me that it was because I asked you to go. Yesterday you were all set to marry someone else. You can't have any interest in me, other than as some sort of substitute, and I have too much self-respect to be that for any man.'

He went on watching her, his mouth a wry line. When she was silent, he gave a little nod. 'You're right, of course, and I apologise—my only excuse is that I've had a bad weekend.'

Sian gave a helpless snort of laughter, then tried to look serious again, but it was no use.

He smiled down at her. 'I lost my temper. It seemed the last straw, for some reason, when you pushed me away and told me to get lost.'

'Your ego couldn't take any more?' she suggested, tongue in cheek.

'Something like that.' He ran a hand over his dishevelled hair and grimaced. 'The past couple of days have been one long nightmare, and I haven't really had a chance to relieve my feelings by smashing anything or raging at anyone—I've had to keep myself on a tight rein because there has been so much to cope with.'

She watched him with understanding, remembering his gentleness with Annette, his patience and sympathy in the hospital.

'It was all bottled up, and I'm sorry it had to explode at you,' Cass finished, offering her his hand in a formal way. 'Will you accept the apology?'

She shook hands without laughing, recognising the sincerity of the gesture. A kiss would have been out of place after what had just happened. The handshake was perfect.

'You know, you're quite formidable when you're in a temper,' he said then, relaxing, and she eyed him disbelievingly.

'I am? What about you?'

He grinned. 'Yes, sorry about that, as I said. I'm afraid I do have a temper, but it's just "sound and fury, signifying nothing". I'm not really dangerous.'

'You had me fooled, then. I was beginning to look around for a blunt instrument to use if you suddenly went for me with murder in mind!'

'Oh, it wasn't murder I had in mind,' he drawled teasingly, and she went pink, which made him laugh again. 'My God, you're a surprising woman! Spitting teeth one minute, blushing the next!' He turned on his heel and strolled towards the front door. 'I'd better go before I get any more ideas.'

Sian followed him, hot-cheeked, and wondering what he meant by that. He said goodnight and added, 'I am sorry, Sian.'

Before she could answer he had gone, and she slowly closed the door, her face confused. He called her surprising! He was a bewildering man, and she didn't know how she felt about him now, but she was disturbed because she had a suspicion that it wasn't going to be easy for her to forget she had ever met him, and as they were never likely to meet again that would have been the wisest thing she could do.

She turned on her answering machine and listened drily to the succession of calls she had had from an increasingly irate Leo, terminating in one that threatened dismissal, decapitation and disaster unless she rang him immediately. Sian turned off the machine and went to bed. She would see Leo tomorrow morning. That was soon enough for her. It would have to be soon enough for Leo, too.

She overslept, exhausted by the events of the weekend, and had to rush her breakfast before dashing to work. She hadn't had time to read the morning papers as usual, but she was only a little late when at last she reached the office. As she walked through the newsroom eyes followed her, people grinned, she caught the subterranean whispers and her teeth met.

They must all know about her involvement with the Cassidy story; they had probably been talking about it all weekend. Sian was grateful that they only knew the public part of the story. They wouldn't have any idea what had happened between her and William Cassidy last night.

'Leo wants you,' one of the other reporters said. The front page of one of their competitors lay open in front of him, and Sian suddenly caught sight of her own face in a huge picture dominating the page.

'What the...' she began, snatching up the paper.

'Yes, it's you,' Carl said with dry amusement. 'And when Leo gets hold of you you're for it. Where do we bury the pieces?'

Sian was frantically skimming the story which went with the photograph. The other papers didn't mention her name or job; they had got this snap of her with Cass outside the hospital the morning after she and Annette had slept at the Cassidy house, and from the way the story had been written the obvious implication was that she was replacing Annette in Cass's life.

'Are you?' asked the other reporter, and Sian looked up dazedly.

'What?'

'The new woman in his life,' Carl said, grinning.

'Go to hell!' Sian said, throwing the paper down and rushing towards Leo's office to assure him that it was a stupid lie, a typical invention of the other paper, and that there was nothing between her and Cass at all. She had to stop Leo making matters worse by embellishing the story in their own pages. He was quite capable of getting someone to write up a follow-up with all sorts of embroidery decorating the first ridiculous lie. She had to stop him.

CHAPTER FIVE

LEO didn't believe a word of it but, when she furiously insisted that there was nothing whatever in the story about her and Cass, he sulkily had to accept that.

'But I want some sort of story,' he said, glowering from his chair. 'Go and knock out a few columns of inside stuff right away.'

'About what? There's nothing to write about, and anyway, I promised . . .'

'Aha!' he triumphantly burst out. 'You promised Cassidy what, exactly? Let me remind you, you work for us. Your first loyalty is to the paper.' Then he paused for thought and cunningly added, 'To your readers, I mean—you owe them the truth, they have a right to know——'

'Know what?' she crossly interrupted. 'The story's cold, Leo. Annette's father had a heart attack, but he's going to make it, and I did the story about Annette and her true love. We can't re-hash yesterday's news.'

'Give us an inside story about how Cassidy's taking it.'

'I wouldn't know,' she lied, and from Leo's cynical face she knew that she wasn't very convincing.

'He didn't make a pass?'

'I told you, no!' Lying to Leo wasn't really lying, because if he was told the truth he wouldn't hesi-

90

tate to use it against her as well as against Cass. In pure self-protection Sian lied, and inwardly had a qualm of sympathy for all the people who had lied to her in the past when she had been trying to dig out facts about them.

'But he made you spend the night at his house!'

'To chaperone Annette!'

Leo made a gruesome face. 'Oh, well, describe the house, then, describe what happened, write anything, but give me a story, damn you!'

She escaped, having promised to do a colour piece on the Cassidy house and how Annette had taken her father's heart attack. Cass wasn't going to like it, but at least he wouldn't be reading columns of overheated prose about this invented relationship between them, she thought. He would have to be thankful about that.

She had to put up with a lot of teasing from her colleagues, but as they all went off to do the stories Leo had sent them to cover Sian was left in peace to write her copy in the office. She was rather suspicious because Leo hadn't detailed her to work on any outside stories, but for the rest of that day she was kept busy writing up agency stories Leo didn't want to put in the paper the way they had come in, usually because they were too bald and Leo wanted them angled for the paper.

It wasn't what Sian was accustomed to doing; it was a job for a sub-editor, in fact, but from the way Leo spoke she realised it was partly intended for a punishment. His other reason for keeping her hanging around the office was less obvious, but she guessed that, too.

Leo wanted her under his eye. He wanted to know if Cass contacted her, or she contacted Cass. Over the weekend, she had vanished and left him without a clue what she was up to, although other papers had reported her presence at the hospital, and with Cass, so Leo had known where she was but had been unable to get hold of her. He wasn't going to let that happen again!

He was still suspicious of her; he knew she hadn't told him the whole truth about her and Cass. He might even guess quite accurately what that truth might be, but he wasn't finding out from her and he knew that, so he was going to keep her where he could watch her. Sian wasn't getting out of his sight again.

Cass must have seen the papers, but he didn't ring and he didn't show up at the newspaper, so as the day wore on Sian became more relieved and Leo grew more morose and accusing.

In the end, he had to let her go home—he had no excuse for keeping her at the office after her shift was over, much as he would have liked to think of one.

She took the underground home. It was raining lightly when she emerged from the station, so she started to run, but hadn't gone far before she noticed the limousine crawling beside her along the kerb. Sian looked casually in that direction at first, then did a double-take as she recognised it.

'Can I give you a lift?' Cass asked, leaning over to talk out of his lowered window.

'You can get into trouble for that, you know!' she said, turning towards the car and trying not to be too pleased to see him.

'For what?' he asked, pulling up to a standstill so that she could slip into the passenger seat.

'Kerb-crawling. A policeman might think you were trying to pick up women.'

'I was—in the singular,' he said, and gave her a wicked, sidelong smile. 'And *you* are very singular.'

She clicked home the seat-belt, feeling oddly at home in the luxurious interior now. 'Dare I ask what you're doing here?'

'Waiting for you,' he coolly admitted. 'I thought you might like to hear the latest news of Annette's father.'

'How is he?' she asked, sobering.

'The hospital are being cautiously optimistic. They say he has a fighting chance.'

'I'm glad.' She threw him a swift glance, then looked away, her heart light. 'How kind of you to go to so much trouble to let me know.'

'Sarcasm is the lowest form of wit,' he said, his mouth twisting upwards, and she laughed. 'I did have another motive for meeting you from work,' Cass added.

'What was that?' she asked blandly.

'I thought it would be nice to have dinner.' He said it very casually, but both of them knew the invitation was far from casual, and Sian took a deep breath, knowing that this was some sort of turning point in her life, in both their lives. She had a dozen good reasons for turning him down, for politely making an excuse and saying goodnight. She knew that if she really wanted to she could end it now, make sure that he never came again. She firmly told herself that that was what she must do.

All she had to do was make him realise how utterly impossible it was for them to see each other again. Taking a deep breath, she asked huskily, 'Did you see the morning papers?'

She expected his face to darken, expected him to start breathing fire and brimstone about the latest gossip, but instead he laughed. 'I did. I must say, your colleagues have very active imaginations.'

Sian was incredulous. She looked at him, searching his face for clues to this extraordinary cheerfulness. It didn't add up when she remembered his rage over the other newspaper stories in the last few days.

'But if we have dinner, if we're seen together again,' she said slowly, 'that will hit the gossip columns, too.'

'I'm counting on it,' he drawled, and that was when the truth dawned on her. It wasn't Cass who was slow on the uptake—it was her. Of course he didn't mind their names being coupled! He was delighted. If the gossip columnists thought he had a new romance, they would concentrate on that and stop harping on about Annette, about his humiliation in being jilted at the very altar. Cass was indifferent about the gossip over himself and Sian—it was mention of Annette that hurt him.

Sian's teeth met. He was using her again, just as ruthlessly as when he had made love to her in her flat, and for exactly the same reason! His ego needed it.

'It doesn't bother you that I'm being gossiped about, too?' she asked bitterly. 'I suppose I'm expected to be flattered to have my name linked with yours?'

'This is your profession,' he said. 'Maybe it's time you found out how it feels to be on the receiving end.'

She looked at him with dislike. 'I don't think I will have dinner, thank you. Will you drop me at my flat, please?'

'No,' he said, putting his foot down on the accelerator and shooting past her flat a moment later, in spite of her angry protests.

'I won't have dinner with you!' she yelled above the roar of the engine. 'Do you hear? I won't get out of the car; I won't have dinner.'

He didn't answer, which made her fidget restlessly. 'Did you hear me?' she asked, and he gave her a silent grin which sent her into positive mania. 'Stop this car, let me out. I'm not having dinner with you and I won't be used in any of your little games.'

Cass laughed, which seemed the last straw. Sinking uselessly back in the seat, Sian gave up talking and concentrated on planning her escape. She would jump out the next time he stopped at a set of traffic lights, and run like hell; he could hardly abandon his car in the street, holding up the rest of the traffic, while he chased her, could he? Could he? She slid a look at him, not sure about that. He was capable of anything.

They were approaching traffic lights now; he was slowing, the lights were red. Sian tensed, ready to move, but with inward fury saw the lights turn amber, then green. Cass picked up speed again and, baffled, she relaxed her muscles.

'What are you plotting, I wonder?' he thought aloud, giving her a probing look before looking back at the road ahead. 'Whatever it is, don't bother, because you owe me for having printed that first story about the wedding. You got your friends excited in the first place, and I'm sorry if it isn't convenient for you to read about yourself in the papers, but there's a rather satisfying irony in it, and you're going to have to put up with it for a little while.'

Sian didn't answer. She sat waiting for the next traffic lights, her eyes leaping with rage.

Then Cass turned up a side street, round a corner and into a mews. The car braked, pulled up, stopped. Sian at once reached for the door, but Cass caught hold of her by the waist and pulled her back. She struggled and sprawled over him, flushed and furious.

'Get your hands off me! I could kill you! Let go, damn you!'

He held her firmly, his hands sliding up her body until they stopped just below her breasts, and Sian was abruptly breathless, shaken. She looked backwards, her head tilted so that his face was inverted above her; oddly unfamiliar, disturbing. The silence between them had a new tension. She heard him breathing, heard herself breathing, her heart banging inside her ribcage.

Sian couldn't have put it into words, she wasn't even sure what it was she felt as the silence elongated and they stared at each other from that new angle, but she knew Cass felt it too, how could he avoid doing so when the very air was charged with electricity?

'Have dinner with me, Sian,' he said at last in a low, husky voice, and she slowly nodded.

She would have said anything to break up that conflict. It was unbearable. While he'd stared down at her she had felt naked, as if everything in her lay in her face for him to read—all her thoughts and emotions visible to him. She had been appalled and, like Eve in the Garden of Eden, she had fled into hiding.

Cass helped her sit up, reversed out of the quiet little cobbled mews, and drove on through the Westminster streets until he parked across the road from a fashionable French restaurant. It was the sort of place where you could guarantee being seen and noted; the media haunted it, watching out for celebrities, and would-be celebrities haunted it, hoping to be noticed.

'I'm not really dressed for a place like that,' Sian wailed, looking down at her simple black and white striped cotton dress.

'Very chic, I'd say,' Cass assured her, firmly walking her across the road.

'Oh, would you?' she muttered. 'What do you know about clothes?'

'I know what I like,' he said with amusement. 'And I like what you're wearing.'

She ran a hand over her blonde hair. 'I look a mess.'

'Stop fishing for compliments!'

'I was doing nothing of the kind!' she protested, turning pink and giving him a furious look.

He paused on the doorstep of the restaurant and looked down at her. 'You look lovely,' he said softly, and Sian was dry-mouthed and silenced.

They sat in the shadowy little bar before they went into the restaurant itself; Cass ordered a Kir for her and a cocktail for himself. Sian was self-conscious, aware that already people were watching them. Press? Or just fellow-diners who recognised them from that morning's papers? Either way, she hated being stared at, and got up.

'I won't be long, I'm going to the powder-room,' she told Cass, as he rose too.

There wasn't much she could do about her dress, but she washed her hot face and renewed her make-up, spent some time doing her blonde hair, sprayed perfume behind her ears and at her wrists, then stared accusingly at her reflection. Why was she here with Cass, in spite of all her brave resolutions about never seeing him again? She knew what he was up to; he had boldly admitted it. He was a user; he had used her shamelessly from the start, and he would go on doing it if she let him. Why was she being such a fool?

The image in the mirror had no answers; it stared back, green eyes far too big and far too bright, too excited for safety. She looked grimly at herself.

'You make me sick, do you know that? You shouldn't be let out on your own.'

The door opened, and another girl came in and looked at her in surprise, then amusement. She had clearly overheard Sian talking to herself.

'It isn't any good, you know!' she said, laughing.

'What isn't?' Sian asked, taken aback.

'Telling yourself off. You never take any notice. Or at least, I don't!' She giggled and Sian smiled before going back to join Cass.

He was leaning back against the velvet-covered seat, his glass in one hand, his face reflective, but as she came towards him his eyes focused on her and roved from her smoothly brushed blonde hair down over her slim figure in the black and white striped dress to her long, shapely legs. It was an openly assessing stare, and Sian bristled under it.

She sat down and gave him a cold look. 'Is our table ready yet?' The sooner this meal was over and she got away, the better she would like it.

'You haven't finished your drink.'

She picked up the glass and drained the pink liquid. 'I have now.'

Cass laughed and swallowed the last of his own drink before getting up. Their table was in an alcove fringed with drooping fern; a private little corner, except that to get to their tables other diners had to walk past them, and each time glanced curiously into the alcove. That apparently didn't bother Cass; he wanted to be seen with her and blandly ignored the stares, but Sian fretted under them, resenting it every time.

The menu had been one long list of very rich food, so she had chosen the simplest things available—tomato salad followed by plainly cooked sole served with a tossed green salad. The tomatoes were thinly sliced, dressed in olive oil and basil; the flavour was delicious. While they ate, Cass talked casually about his work, his family, his home, and Sian listened without saying much.

'Am I boring you?' he asked, sounding aggrieved, and she looked up.

'No.' Their eyes met and she smiled suddenly, seeing the expression he wore. 'Not at all. I'm a reporter, remember. I'm always curious about other people. In fact, I'm curious about everything.'

'Hmm,' he said, eyeing her. 'I thought you were being monosyllabic because you were bored rigid. I keep forgetting your job. You're a dangerous woman to have around, aren't you? I'm telling you far too much about myself.'

Before she answered that, a man strolled past the alcove and turned his head to look at them. Becoming aware of him, Sian glanced his way at the same moment, and each recognised the other in shock.

'Louis!' She sounded breathless, almost guilty, and went pink.

'Sian! What on earth are you doing here?' Louis walked over and stood there, giving Cass a hard stare which wasn't friendly. He got a cold, narrow-eyed look in return.

'How are you?' Sian asked, her presence of mind deserting her at this unexpected meeting. Their last meeting had been so violent; each had said things that had hurt and were best forgotten, and Sian hadn't quite got over either their affair or the abrupt ending of it. She wasn't still in love with Louis; she never had been deeply in love, but she had cared about him, and his angry accusations had been disturbing. He had demanded that she choose him or her job—and in asking that he had focused her attention on a painful truth. She had had to realise that her career and her love-life were in opposition, and might always be incompatible unless she found some very special man who could take the sort of life she led, the sort of woman she was, and that it wouldn't be Louis; it might never be anyone.

That hadn't been a very happy realisation, and she was flushed and upset by seeing Louis again.

'I'm fine,' he said oddly. 'I can see you are.'

There was a sting to that, and he underlined it by giving Cass another cold look. Sian realised then that Louis must have read the morning papers, too, and he probably believed what he had read. He thought she had started an affair with Cass, and seeing them here tonight made it certain. Louis might have chucked her over, but he resented the fact that she had got over him so soon and found another man, especially one as wealthy as William Cassidy.

Louis would have sulked over any man she was with, even though she didn't belong to him any more. He had always been a possessive man, as well as a selfish one.

It was odd, because he was very good-looking and had a lot of charm. You wouldn't think he needed to be possessive; women had always liked Louis, and a lot of girls had let Sian see they envied her when she'd gone out with him.

'How's the job?' he asked with a faint sneer, looking at Cass again. Did he expect Cass to resent her career the way he did? Or was he hinting that she was using Cass to further her career?

'Terrific,' she said coolly, aware of Cass watching them both, his grey eyes frozen but observant. He hadn't said a word, and she hadn't tried to introduce Louis. She didn't think Cass wanted to meet him.

'We ought to get together again soon,' Louis said, unbelievably, and she just looked at him, her green eyes wide with derision. Why had he said that?

'I'll give you a buzz,' he said. 'See you.'

She stared after him, still baffled, then the waiter came to take her plate away and looked reproachfully at her uneaten food.

'Sorry, I'm not as hungry as I thought,' she apologised, and he removed her plate with an offended smile.

'So, who was that?' Cass asked while they waited for their next course. 'A fellow scribe?'

'Sorry, I'd have introduced you if I thought you wanted to meet him,' she lied, and was given a dry, disbelieving look.

'What made you think I didn't want to?'

She made flustered noises. 'Well...I...'

'I got the idea he was more than just a colleague, though,' said Cass, and her eyes slid away, her skin burnt.

'I can't think why you should...'

'I thought he was jealous,' Cass coolly continued over her stammering.

'Jealous?' she laughed, a little wildly and unconvincingly. 'Good heavens, no! Jealous of what?'

'Of me,' said Cass, and she laughed some more.

'Of you? Of course not.'

'He certainly didn't like finding us together,' he said, watching her closely.

Sian shot him a look, then away. 'I haven't seen him for ages,' she volunteered in the hope of stopping the discussion there. A hope misplaced.

'Why not?' enquired Cass, and she opened her mouth and closed it again, daunted by the prospect of explaining.

'Oh, you know the way it goes,' she offered.

'No, tell me,' he invited softly.

Sian shrugged helplessly. 'Well, it didn't...'

'Work out?' suggested Cass, and she jumped at the words.

'Work out—exactly.'

'Why not?'

'Why not?' she repeated, floundering again. 'Well, it just didn't.'

'He's not bad-looking,' he thought aloud, his tone tolerant.

'He's very good-looking,' corrected Sian, to be fair to Louis.

'Hmm,' Cass said, frowning. 'And he obviously still fancies you. So why did you split up? A quarrel?'

'In a way,' she capitulated, realising he meant to find out. 'He didn't like my job and gave me an ultimatum—him or my job. So we split up.'

'He must be a fool,' said Cass. 'What sort of ultimatum is that? What else did he expect you to do? You're well rid of him. I admire your taste.'

She looked blankly at him.

'You can't have cared tuppence about him or you wouldn't have chosen your job,' Cass said and she glared at him.

'How I felt about him had nothing to do with it! I just couldn't see why I should give up my job—for him, or any man.'

Cass smiled, his mouth crooked. 'That's what I meant. You obviously weren't that crazy about him in the first place, or he wouldn't have needed to hand out ridiculous ultimatums.'

She laughed scornfully. 'Oh, I see! You believe a woman in love loses all interest in everything else, especially a career? How old-fashioned can you get?'

'You can't compartmentalise love,' he murmured softly. 'It takes over everything else in your life, even your work, whether you're a man or a woman—and there's nothing old-fashioned about that, it's as up to date as tomorrow morning's paper.'

Sian gave a guilty start, remembering that she had written a colour piece about his home and family, and the aftermath of Annette's father's heart attack. Only a few hours and he would be reading it—and how would he react then?

Cass looked shrewdly into her confused green eyes, his brows going up. 'What now? Why are you looking at me like that?'

Flushed, she took refuge in temper. 'Stop trying to read my mind, damn you!'

'Are you afraid I can?' he asked in a lowered tone, and with a start she realised she was; she actually suspected he could tell from her face what she was thinking.

'No!' she said, far too quickly, with far too much emphasis, and he laughed in a distinctly satisfied way, but then their dessert arrived and Sian was able to steer the conversation into less personal channels. All the same, she was disturbed as he drove her home later. During dinner, they had come closer; far too close. She really felt that she was getting to know him and that he knew a lot about her, and even that he could get through her defences and understand what made her tick—and that was very worrying.

Seeing Louis again had vividly reminded her of the dangers of caring about a man. They became possessive, jealous, demanding—they wanted more than you cared to give, and you ended up getting hurt because of the impossible demands of both your man and your career. She still had a world to conquer; she was ambitious and wanted to climb in her career. She couldn't do that and tie herself to a man.

Then she glanced sideways and in the yellow glare of a street light saw Cass—his hard face in profile to her, his eyes hooded and his mouth a firm line. She saw more than that—she saw the gloss of power over him, the strength of his background, his wealth and influence.

And she laughed at herself. She was letting her imagination run riot. Cass wasn't seriously interested in her. He had taken her out tonight to make capital out of the latest gossip—to make people forget how he had been jilted, to soothe his ego over the humiliation of being left at the altar. She was just a means to an end, and if he seemed to know what she was thinking it was only because he was a clever, shrewd man, a skilled negotiator and manipulator who knew human beings, not merely women.

While she was arguing with herself over whether she wanted him or not, Cass was blissfully unaware of her. If he knew what she was thinking he would laugh at her, and she would deserve it. For a while, she had forgotten Annette—but he had wanted to marry Annette, and he must still be in love with her or he wouldn't have gone to so much trouble for her, even after she had left him at the altar.

Sian turned her head away, biting her lip. What a fool you are! she told herself. Grow up!

Cass pulled up outside her flat and turned to smile at her. 'Thank you for a very pleasant evening.'

'I hope it achieved what you wanted it to achieve,' Sian said tartly, and he laughed, as though not hearing the angry note in her voice.

'I saw one gossip columnist in the restaurant and I know he saw us. One is enough.'

'More than enough, I'd say,' Sian muttered, turning to get out of the car, but Cass caught her shoulder and casually pulled her back towards him before she knew what he was up to.

As he bent to kiss her she wildly hit out, meaning only to push him away. The sound of the slap as it landed on his cheek made both of them jump, but especially Sian, even more surprised than he was, since she hadn't intended to slap his face.

There was a dangerous pause, while she stared, aghast, at the spreading redness on his skin, and he stared back at her as if he couldn't believe she had actually dared to hit him.

Then he slammed her backwards against the seat, and kept her there with the weight of his body while he began to kiss her forcibly, his mouth angry and bruising. Sian struggled uselessly; he was far too strong for her and the kiss was no pleasure.

'I hate you, stop it!' she tried to say, but the words were muffled by his hard mouth.

Frustration and rage made her shake; a tear trickled from under her lids and then another. She wept with fury because she understood why he was so violent. It had nothing to do with her per-sonally—her slap had simply reminded him of Annette and his humiliation when she had walked out on him. He was taking revenge on Sian as the nearest female and she bitterly resented it.

At last, breathing thickly, Cass lifted his head and she glared up at him. 'You make me sick,' she said, and he turned pale himself.

'I'm sorry, I lost my temper.'

'Don't bother to make excuses,' Sian said shakily, white and tear-stained and in a mood to bite him. 'Just let me out of here before I throw up. I've had enough of you and your damned ego! Why should I have to carry the can for Annette? It wasn't my fault she walked out on you, and I don't want to listen to any more of your explanations or apologies. I just want to get away from you and never set eyes on you again.'

He opened his mouth, then shut it. A moment later Sian was bolting across the pavement to her flat, and Cass was driving away with a roar of power, his tail lights vanishing, although she didn't look back to watch. She went straight to bed in a state of deep depression. That was the last time she would ever see Cass!

CHAPTER SIX

SIAN WAS optimistic. After a very bad night, she was eating her muesli and keeping an eye on the clock because she still had to do her make-up before she left for work, when the doorbell went. Sian had no premonition. She thought it must be the girl next door, wanting to borrow milk for her cornflakes, or the postman with a parcel he couldn't slip through the letterbox. At that hour of the morning she wasn't expecting Cass, and when she saw him on the doorstep she stared in surprise.

He was clutching a newspaper and he was in one of his rages; his eyes glittered at her and he was breathing like a bull about to charge.

'And I was stupid enough to tell myself I could trust you!' he said, waving the paper at her. 'How could you do it? Don't you have any decency?'

Sian looked at the newspaper; it was her own. She had forgotten writing the colour piece and flushed.

'Look, I'm sorry...'

'Don't say it,' he bit out. 'Last night you told me you didn't want to hear any more apologies—well, that goes for me, too. You wrote about my private life, my family, my home! And then you called me a user! What the hell are you?'

A door opened across the landing and Sian took hold of his shirt front and pulled him into her flat. Slamming the door, she hissed at him, 'If I hadn't agreed to write that, my editor would have got someone else to do a far more personal piece. He wanted something along the lines of the stories in the other papers.' She stared pointedly at him. 'If you get my meaning!'

Cass ran a hand uncertainly through his dark hair, still scowling. 'Oh, I see. Well...you're so damn plausible, that's the trouble. I'm never sure where I am with you, or if you're telling me the truth.'

'I am,' she said indignantly.

'Maybe you are, but I keep finding myself telling you things I certainly wouldn't like to read in the morning paper, and it bothers me the way you ferret things out of me.'

'I don't ferret anything!' Sian said, glowering back. 'If you read that piece carefully, you'll see what pains I went to not to write anything a good reporter couldn't find out from a cuttings library.'

'You described the interior of my home!' he snapped. 'Where could you find out details like that, except from being there?'

Eyeing him scornfully, Sian asked, 'Do you remember allowing an interior design magazine to use your home for a big double-page feature?'

His face changed. 'Oh.'

'Yes, oh,' she repeated, eyes cold.

'I'd forgotten that.'

'Well, maybe next time you'll check your information before you come accusing people of double-crossing you,' said Sian, opening the front door again. 'Goodbye, Mr Cassidy.'

He leaned on the door and forced it shut again. 'Sian, I'm sorry.'

'I thought we agreed we were both sick of apologies? Would you mind going? I was eating a peaceful breakfast when you arrived.'

'I was eating a peaceful breakfast until I saw this and promptly got indigestion.' He glanced into the kitchen. 'I would love a cup of coffee, and maybe a slice of toast and marmalade.'

'Go away,' said Sian.

'You look pale,' he suddenly commented, staring, then said, 'Oh, no—I see what it is, you aren't wearing any make-up. What pale skin you have naturally—your eyelids look almost transparent.'

'Don't stand so close,' she said huskily, and bolted into the kitchen because having him merely inches away was nerve-racking.

He followed and coolly sat down at the table. 'I'm hungry again. Reading that article made me lose my appetite.'

She poured him coffee and made him toast in grim silence, then sat down and finished her muesli.

Cass ate his toast while she pretended to read the morning paper he had brought with him. 'I suppose you have to read all the papers to keep abreast of what the opposition is doing,' he said and she made a vague, agreeing noise behind the paper.

'But you haven't seen the other papers this morning?' he continued, and she made an equally vague noise that meant no, she had not.

Cass said, 'Ah,' and she stiffened, suddenly picking up a note in his voice that she wasn't happy with. She peered over the top of the paper and saw him grinning to himself. She wasn't happy with that, either.

'What's amusing you?' she asked suspiciously.

Cass finished his coffee and leaned back in his chair, his hands linked behind his head and his grey eyes mocking.

'You'll find out. Can I give you a lift to work?'

She was tempted to refuse, but that would have been cutting off her nose to spite her face, and a lift would be a luxury, especially as she had now been delayed and might otherwise be late, so she said coolly that that would be very nice.

'I won't be more than five minutes getting ready,' she assured him, making for the bathroom.

'Famous last words,' said Cass tolerantly, but she was back before he expected her. She had given her face a delicate make-up: a film of very light foundation and then a gentle brushing with powder, shimmering blue on her lids, then the merest touch of mascara on her lashes, and finally a soft rose-pink on her mouth. Her mirror showed her the image she wanted—her blonde hair framed a coolly sophisticated face, and she felt she would be able now to keep Cass at a distance without losing her temper or her dignity.

He stood up when she came back, and then paused to stare. She pretended not to realise he was staring. 'Can we go, then?' She would have to leave the muddle of breakfast things until she got back tonight, she thought.

'Oh. Yes. Of course,' he said in an oddly disjointed, husky way, and her heart turned over and over, like a salmon leaping upstream. The sensation was peculiar and left her breathless as they went out to his car. She couldn't think of anything to say all the way to her office. Cass seemed abstracted, too, and dropped her outside the building

with a curt nod as she got out, but although he
didn't say anything she felt him staring after her as
she walked across the pavement and through the
swing doors. Sian was wearing a straight-cut blue
silk dress: tight-waisted and clinging. Every step she
took, her body swayed inside the dress, forced to
that motion by the style of the dress and her high
heels. She had worn the dress before without being
so tensely aware of being watched, but for some
inexplicable reason Cass's stare made her throat
tighten and her skin burn.

The receptionist in the lobby was reading a paper;
over the top of it she suddenly saw Sian and her
eyes rounded. She audibly giggled. Sian looked hard
at her and at the paper she was reading. Her heart
sank. What had the other papers printed to make
Cass drop meaningful hints and this girl giggle?

She soon found out. Leo had them all on his desk
and furiously read bits out to Sian in between gob-
bling like an enraged turkey cock about loyalty, and
did she really want her job or was she about to
become Mrs Cassidy and give up work altogether?

'Look, he took me out to dinner—big deal,' Sian
said boldly, chin up. 'So what? It's all a storm in
a teacup, and I didn't ring in with a story because
I'm not using myself as copy, for you or anyone.'

Leo showed her his teeth and she backed. They
were a horrible sight. 'Do I have to put a reporter
on your tail?' he threatened, and she blenched.

'You can't do that! I work for you!'

'You're also providing all our rivals with some
Technicolor copy, while we get zilch,' Leo growled.

'Be reasonable, Leo!' she pleaded.

'I *am* being reasonable. I ought to fire you, but I'll give you another chance. From now on, I want to get any stuff about you and Cassidy before the rest of Fleet Street hears a word. Or you are out.'

She was infuriated. 'What do you want me to do? Issue a minute-by-minute diary of my social engagements in future?'

The sarcasm was water off an editor's back. 'Yes,' Leo said. 'If Cassidy's involved, yes.' He waved a lordly hand. 'Get back to work. What do you think we pay you for?'

'I'm beginning to wonder,' she told him bitterly. 'I thought I was here to report the news, not make it.'

'Quite the wit,' he sneered.

'Talking about the news, why aren't I being sent out of town on stories?' she attacked, and he looked shifty.

'I don't organise the office. I suppose it's your turn to stay in London.'

Sian didn't believe a word of it. They were deliberately keeping her in town so that she could see Cass and they could follow her romantic entanglement, along with the rest of the media. Giving Leo a murderous look, she stormed back to her desk.

She was out of the office for most of the day on a London story, but late in the afternoon she was working at her screen, tidying up her copy before sending it down to the subs, when Leo sent for her again.

'It's urgent,' the messenger said when Sian made furious faces and doggedly went on checking her copy on the computer screen.

She set her teeth and despatched her copy with a gesture of resignation before getting up. What did Leo want now?

Leo's secretary gave her a quick signal, and she paused before going into his office. 'What is it, Lucy?'

His secretary leaned over to whisper. 'He's got someone with him...Mrs Cassidy!' Her saucer eyes held a mixture of pity, fascination and shock, and Sian went red, then white.

'Mrs Cassidy?' She had read a great deal about William Cassidy over the past few days; she had ransacked the cuttings library and references books for every detail about him, but nowhere had she read that he had ever married. 'Mrs Cassidy?' she said again, frowning and feeling faintly sick.

The office door opened and Leo looked out, perhaps having heard her voice. He gave her an urgent beckoning of the head, his hand winding her forward at the same moment. Aloud, he said, 'Ah, there you are, Sian!' with a horrible enthusiasm meant for the consumption of whoever was in his office, rather than for Sian herself. 'Come along in!' he added, grimacing at her out of sight of his visitor.

'"Will you walk into my parlour? said the spider to the fly,"' Sian murmured, and his secretary giggled.

'What did you say?' scowled Leo, and she walked past him, smiling sweetly at him without answering.

Her eyes fled across the room to find the other occupant, and stopped dead as she saw the woman sitting by the desk. One thing was obvious. This wasn't Cass's ex-wife. She was far too old, her hair white, even though it was still copious and very long. She wore it piled high upon her head, pinned there with an ornate Spanish comb, giving her a dignified air which matched the black dress she wore: elegant and discreet, with a touch of white lace at collar and cuffs. She wore diamonds, too, though; in her ears and on her hands. They flashed blue fire as she held out one hand to Sian.

'You must be Sian. I'm so pleased to meet you.'

'Sian, this is Mrs Cassidy,' Leo said, bustling over.

The older woman turned blindingly blue eyes on him and smiled. 'Would you mind if we had a few moments alone? Would it inconvenience you if we borrowed your office for a few moments?'

'No, of course not,' Leo said fulsomely, backing like someone in the presence of royalty, bowing his way to the door. 'Be my guest...excuse me...'

Sian watched him go, then looked curiously at the white-haired woman still clasping her hand. She was either someone very important and powerful, or she had the personality to knock Leo off his feet. Sian had never seen him so humble and awed. The door closed behind him and Mrs Cassidy smiled at her.

'Now we can talk,' she said, and Sian warily smiled back.

'What are we going to talk about?' she politely enquired, her green eyes reserved.

'Cass.' The older woman's voice was half amused.

Sian knew that, of course; there could be no other reason for her to be there, but Sian knew his parents were dead.

'I'm not quite clear who...'

'I am? I'm sorry, my dear—I suppose I thought you would guess. I'm Lorna Cassidy, William's aunt.'

'Aunt?' Sian was surprised by that; Cass hadn't said he had an aunt.

'By marriage, of course. My husband was his father's brother. They are all dead now, unhappily; I'm the last of my generation in the family. I didn't have any children of my own, and I think of William almost as a son, especially since his mother died.'

'Oh, I see,' Sian said, still wary because she suspected the other woman's motives in being here. Was she about to be asked to stop seeing Cass? Or threatened? Or even blackmailed? After all she had learnt about the Cassidy family, nothing would surprise her. No doubt Magdalena had asked her aunt to visit the newspaper and put the fear of God into Sian! Well, she needn't bother. None of them need worry, the mighty Cassidy clan! Sian was no danger to them; it was still Annette Cass loved, and Sian had too much self-respect to let him go on using her either for amusement or as a smokescreen.

'Like everyone else, I've been reading the papers,' Mrs Cassidy said.

Sian nodded without comment. Of course she had! Why else would she be here?

'I'm grateful to you, Sian. May I call you Sian, by the way? Such a lovely name, simple but delightful. I was horrified when my sister-in-law chose to call her little girl Magdalena, but then Enid was always one for going over the top. Magda takes after her in that. My brother-in-law chose the boys' names; good solid English names, so much more sensible.'

Sian was a little confused, but smiled. There seemed to be no need to comment; Mrs Cassidy didn't pause for more than an instant. 'Do sit down, Sian. We can't talk while you loom over me.'

Sian backed to a chair and sat, her hands in her lap.

Mrs Cassidy considered her shrewdly. 'Being jilted at the last minute like that was a terrible blow to William's pride, of course, but I think he was lucky. If he had married Annette, it would have been far worse for him in the long run, that's my opinion—not that he asked for it, but then William never takes any notice of what anyone else thinks.'

'I see you know him well!'

'And I see that you do,' his aunt nodded, smiling. 'I'm very curious. I have been ever since I first heard about you. I couldn't quite make up my mind whether William wanted to kill you or see more of you.'

Sian turned crimson and looked away, her heart racing.

'Whatever it was, your effect on him was interesting,' said Mrs Cassidy. 'And the media are obviously intrigued, too.'

'That was his idea,' Sian confessed hurriedly. 'He wanted them to think that we . . . that . . .'

'Yes, I see; typical. He's horribly intelligent—it can be quite annoying.'

'That's true,' said Sian, struck by the observation.

'So he wants the press to think there's a romance between you?' Mrs Cassidy thought aloud, smiling.

'Well, then, let's put some more fuel on the flames, shall we?'

Sian stared, bewildered.

'Will you spend the weekend at my home, Sian?' asked Mrs Cassidy. 'Of course, William will be there. I'm giving a garden party on Saturday in aid of charity, and you and William will have a much bigger audience than usual for your little soap opera. That you're staying with his aunt should be a very convincing twist, and they'll soon forget Annette and the wedding that never happened.'

Stunned, Sian didn't know what to say. She got a friendly smile as Mrs Cassidy rose.

'I . . . it's very kind of you . . . but . . .'

'Talk it over with William,' his aunt said, on her way to the door.

Leo was hovering outside, no doubt trying to eavesdrop. Sian didn't think he had heard much, though, because he had a frustrated look as Mrs Cassidy swept past, giving him a gracious nod.

'Please come, Sian,' she said over her shoulder as she went. 'It should be an eventful weekend.'

When she had vanished into the lift, Leo grabbed Sian and hustled her back into his office. 'What was all that about? Weekend? What did she mean?'

Sian detached herself and rubbed her arm where he had held it. 'You don't know your own strength! I shall want danger money if you do that again.'

He glowered. 'Oh, sorry, sorry—what did she want?'

'She invited me to stay for the weekend, as it happens,' Sian told him in a lofty tone, secretly amused by his excitement.

'Well,' he said, rubbing his hands together. 'This is one scoop the others don't get. Now, listen, I don't want it getting out. Don't tell a living soul.' He sat down behind his desk, frowning. 'I'll let Paul cover it, of course—the gossip column should have it. Could you get him into the house?'

'Are you out of your mind? I only just met the woman, why should she let me bring gossip columnists into her home? And anyway, this has gone far enough—who cares if I stay with William Cassidy's family or not? Nobody's interested.'

'Oh, yes, they are!' Leo protested loudly, red in the face. 'That drama at the wedding made him big news, and you helped do it. A romance between the two of you makes great reading. His publicity people have worked like slaves for years to get his name into the papers on one pretext or another— he can't complain now just because it doesn't suit him. You can't pick and choose your publicity. If you've made yourself a public figure, you have to take what is thrown at you.'

Sian had said all that herself on many previous occasions, about other people. She had never expected to be on the receiving end, or to see it from this less comfortable angle.

Leo calmed down a little when she was silent. Leaning back, he openly assessed her from head to foot. 'Mind you, I can't quite see . . .'

'What?' she asked, bristling.

'Oh, nothing,' he said hastily, confused by her belligerence.

'What he sees in me?' accused Sian, and he made horrified noises, shaking his head.

'Good heavens, no, of course not—I mean, why shouldn't he fancy you? A lot of men like blondes, and you aren't too bad. I mean, you're very pretty, of course, I'm sure a lot of men ... well, some in the office have said ... that is ...' He broke off, breathing heavily, red about the neck. 'I don't know what I mean! You've got me in a state now.'

Sian laughed and told him, 'Serves you right! And I am not smuggling Paul into Mrs Cassidy's house, nor am I writing a story about my weekend with the Cassidy family.' She made for the door and Leo bellowed behind her.

'You'll do as you're told or find another job ...'
Sian slammed the door without replying.

CHAPTER SEVEN

SIAN expected to hear from Cass again before too long, and sure enough he rang her that evening. Sian had been on tenterhooks ever since she'd got back to her flat, waiting for a ring at the doorbell, but it was almost nine in the evening when the phone made her jump out of her chair, and she was so startled that she stared at it numbly for a while before running to snatch it up.

'Hello?'

'Sian?'

His voice sounded far too familiar and her knees went weak. 'Oh, hello,' she said, swallowing and checking hurriedly on her reflection in the window nearby, as if he could actually see her. She had spent some time after getting back from work in making herself look good. Just in case he came round, she had thought defiantly in excuse, because she wasn't planning on going out and had no real reason for dressing carefully, but Cass wasn't catching her unprepared again, so she had put on a pale green linen dress which gave her a cool, contained air. At least if he did appear she would be ready to deal with him.

'How are you?' he asked, as if they hadn't met for weeks, and strangely enough she felt that, too. It seemed a long, long time since breakfast.

'Fine,' she said without betraying that, because he was capable of using the knowledge against her, and Sian did not intend to let him guess he had any effect on her at all. 'What do you want now?' she added crisply.

'Are you in one of your aggressive moods again?' he asked, and laughed, as though she amused him. 'A pity I can't be there to deal with you.'

'Deal with me?' she repeated irately, and he laughed again.

'But I've had to go to Glasgow.'

Sian immediately felt depressed. 'Oh,' she said when he paused for comment, and he went on, his tone wry.

'Business will keep me up here until Friday at the earliest, but I'm going to get to my aunt's place for the weekend if I have to move heaven and earth. You'll be there, won't you?'

Glumly, she said she didn't know, she wasn't sure.

'Promise me!' he said, and she scowled, although he wouldn't see that, either.

'Just so that you can keep the gossip columns happy? Why should I?'

'Why are you so cross?' he asked, his voice hardening, too. 'What's happened?'

She didn't want him to start guessing, to work out that for some peculiar reason she was feeling low because he had gone away.

'Nothing's happened,' she said, forcing a brightness into her voice. 'I'm not cross, not at all. But I do have a life of my own, you know, and you and your insistence on a romantic smokescreen aren't making my life too easy at the moment.'

There was a silence, then he asked tersely, 'Is this all about that guy?'

'Guy? What guy?' She was bewildered.

'The one we ran into in the restaurant.'

'Oh, Louis!' She was at once embarrassed and it sounded in her voice. 'No, of course not.'

'Hmm,' said Cass. 'Sure about that?'

His pressure made her snap. 'What's it to do with you, anyway—even if it was Louis that I was thinking about? I've helped you out to distract the other papers and stop them writing about Annette, but there is a limit. I have a right to a private life of my own.'

'Very well,' Cass said shortly. 'I accept that, but will it hurt to spend a weekend with my aunt? One more favour, then I promise I won't ask again.'

She sighed audibly. 'Oh, all right.'

'Thank you. I'll see you at the weekend, then. Goodnight.'

The click made her start; she put the phone down herself and stood at the window looking at the darkening sky, feeling melancholy, and angry with herself because there was no reason why she should feel that way. A week ago, she hadn't known a thing about William Cassidy; she had been busy every waking hour out on the water down at Poole, sailing and enjoying the sun and wind. Her mind had been carefree. She had put behind her all the anger, uncertainty and confusion she had gone through when she and Louis had split up. She hadn't been in love, of course, but breaking up had been painful, all the same, and once she was over it she had told herself it would be a long, long time before she got tangled up with another man. She had been so sure that she had learnt her lesson, yet here she was in just a few days swinging wildly between inexplicable highs and lows, and all because of a man she hardly knew!

She had never thought of herself as weak-willed or man-mad. In fact, until now, she had always been able to put her career first—why else had she quarrelled with Louis? He had known he came a poor second and he had resented it—but where William Cassidy was concerned it was always her job that seemed to be running second and Cass who got his way, and Sian was baffled and bewildered.

What's the matter with you? she asked herself, prowling around her shadowy flat and feeling more lonely than she had ever felt in her life.

He snaps his fingers and you come running— why? He asks you to let yourself be used as a smokescreen to fool your own colleagues—and you meekly do it. He rings to say he's at the other end of the country and you sink into a black depression.

Glowering into the mirror, she asked her reflection, 'What's wrong with you lately? How does he talk you into it? What hold has he got over you?'

But her green eyes evaded their own reflection, slid aside guiltily, because she didn't need to ask the questions, she knew the answer in her heart, even if she wished she didn't.

It was very late before she fell asleep, and she dreamed all night; in the morning she was shadowy-eyed and her head ached. Worse, she remembered dreams, and her face was hot whenever she thought about them.

She hadn't known that her imagination was so powerful or so vivid; she wished she could forget the dreams, but they hung around her mind like smoke, the fumes sweet and suffocating.

The one positive side of it all was that she could go into the paper next morning and tell Leo that Cass had gone away and she would not be seeing him that week. Leo was suspicious at first. 'Oh, yeah? Where has he gone?'

'Glasgow,' she triumphantly informed him, and the grey reality of the destination convinced him.

'Glasgow?'

'Glasgow,' she repeated, watching his face fall.

Leo looked over the other papers, drumming his fingers on the desk. 'They all have columns on you and Cassidy! What did you two do last night?'

'I don't know what he did,' Sian said coldly. 'I went home, watched TV and went to bed.' She paused, meeting Leo's eyes. 'Alone,' she added in an icy voice.

'That's not what it says in the *Echo*.'

'They're lying rats.'

'That's a fact,' Leo said, laughing. 'Oh, well, you'll be seeing him this weekend, won't you?'

'Possibly.'

Leo glared. 'You told me...'

'Oh, yes, I will see him,' Sian said on a sigh of irritation.

'And you won't tell a soul?'

'Not a soul.'

'And you'll write the piece yourself?'

'Yes.'

He let her go, then, and Sian beat a retreat with a face like thunder, for the first time in her life wondering if she had picked the right career. This wasn't what she had gone into journalism to do— she hated gossip columns and trivia, she hated chitchat and back-biting and bedroom whispers.

She wanted to write about the real world out there; she liked travelling, meeting new people all the time, uncovering corruption in local councils, hearing stories of courage and kindness, human grit and self-sacrifice. That was the ordinary world she had been dealing with—William Cassidy and his affairs were the tinsel of newspapers. Why else had he employed a whole team of publicists to get his company and himself into the media? Leo was right when he said that Cass deserved what was happening; he had invited the press into his life, he couldn't turn round now and kick them out.

She had only just sat down at her desk when she got a phone call. 'A person-to-person call for you,' the operator on the newspaper switchboard said in her flat, bored voice. 'Will you take it?'

Sian's heart beat fast and hard. Dry-mouthed, she asked, 'Who's calling?'

'A Mrs Jennifer Bush from a Poole exchange.'

Sian's traitorous heart slowed again. 'Oh,' she said, then, 'Yes, put her through, will you?'

Jenny sounded breathless. 'Hello, Sian.'

'Hi, Jen—how are you? Anything wrong?'

'My neighbour just showed me yesterday's paper,' Jenny said, and Sian pulled a face.

'Oh.'

'Sian, what's going on?'

'Nothing, Jen—don't get excited. Its all nonsense, honestly.'

'But you never even mentioned him!'

'Look, take no notice of anything you read in the papers. I barely know the man—they're making it all up.'

Jen wasn't easy to convince, and Sian asked her urgently, 'You won't mention this to anyone else, will you? I mean, if my parents should get in touch, or anyone from the family? If they hear about it and ring you, tell them what I said, it's all invention.'

Her parents were in New Zealand, visiting her elder brother, and had been there for months, but Sian was used to them being away for long periods because her father had been in the Air Force, often based overseas, and Sian had gone to school in England, boarding for months at a time and only seeing her parents during the long summer vacations. She had learnt to be independent very early; she had learnt how to be tough and think for herself, and those lessons had stood her in good stead when she became a reporter.

Sian knew that her parents wouldn't worry about her if they heard that she was seeing William Cassidy, but she didn't want to face probing questions from anyone, and her family might be made curious by the newspaper gossip.

The rest of the week was uneventful. Sian worked in the office, or was sent out on stories, mostly around London, although once she got as far as Brighton, and spent a wistful afternoon by the sea. When she phoned in her copy, she strolled around the town, admired the Prince Regent's palace with its domes and cupolas glittering in the sun, like something out of an Arabian Nights' fairy-tale, but didn't go in because she preferred to walk by the sea. A veil of mist hung far out over the milky horizon; the sky held all shades of gentle colour from lavender and grey, and the light was tremulous, shifting; now in sun, now overcast, matching Sian's low-key mood.

She knew something irrevocable had happened to her. She might joke with friends as usual, argue and swap professional chitchat, manage her working day with her old efficiency, but she wasn't the same person she had been a week ago. Her world had spun helplessly into a new orbit, she was in hiatus, waiting—but for what?

She couldn't bear even to think about it. It was irrational, but she kept hoping that, if she ignored it, it would go away, this strange, drifting, volatile mood. She had been quite happy with her life. She didn't want anything to change. Why was this happening to her?

On the Friday, the pulse of time altered and she found herself watching the clock, nervously anticipating, wondering if Cass would get back, working out the route by which she would drive to his aunt's house in Buckinghamshire. She had had a note from Mrs Cassidy, confirming the invitation and suggesting when she should arrive. A hand-drawn map had been helpfully included, and Sian thought she shouldn't have much trouble finding the house.

She promised Leo that she would phone in some copy that weekend; at least giving a story about the garden party, which, as it was for charity, was presumably very much a public event. Since Mrs Cassidy had cheerfully stressed that the press would be there, Sian saw no reason why she shouldn't do a piece on that.

She left London at five-thirty and took some time to disentangle herself from the usual homeward-bound traffic jam, heavier than usual since it was the start of the weekend. Eventually, though, she was out of the suburbs and driving through the green belt surrounding London: a half-rural, half-suburban landscape. Sian much preferred the Hampshire countryside in which Cass lived.

At last, though, she began to drive through a richer landscape: green and fertile, softly folded meadows and wheatfields, round hills and gentle valleys in which lay old cottages of faded red brick or black and white Tudor timbering, set in cottage gardens of peonies and red rambling roses climbing round the door, gold and white sweet-scented honeysuckle flung everywhere over wall and fences. The colours assaulted the senses: delphiniums in deep blue spikes, clove-smelling double pinks, huge white cabbage roses, glorious, glowing orange marigolds. Summer hung there in delirious riot, and as twilight began to descend birds flew calling across the deep-sunk lanes through which she drove; there was a heavy, damp sweetness from the woods— grass and wild garlic, hogweed and woodbine.

Sian drove slowly, her eyes darting everywhere. She didn't know this part of England and had to keep consulting the map she had open on the passenger seat beside her.

Drawing up at a crossroads in the middle of a village she tried to read the ancient signpost. A white-flannelled cricket game was still in progress. Across the smooth green the pale figures ran to and from the wickets. Sian sat listening to those archetypal English sounds—so much a part of summer— the little thud of the ball hitting the bat, the running feet, the sleepy desultory clapping, the voice raised in protest, the clatter of teacups from the little

wooden pavilion where the women were washing
up during these closing stages of the lazy ritual.

Sian was in no hurry to reach the end of her
journey. That might mean facing Cass. Worse, it
might mean facing herself, and she was reluctant
to do that, but at last she drove on, as the signpost
directed, along the left-hand lane, narrow, de-
serted, the hawthorn hedges on each side, and below
them ditches and wild flowers for which so far the
bureaucrats had not given orders of extinction. No
doubt weedkillers would spray them soon, but as
yet they blew softly in the warm summer breeze—
creamy white sprays of wild parsley, pink campion,
scarlet poppy, spotted foxglove and tall yellow
toadflax. Sian was delighted to see them, and kept
looking aside at them, fascinated.

That was why she didn't see the other car come
racing round the corner. One minute she was alone
in the lane; the next a long, white sports car flashed
past with a screech of tyres, shaving the side of her
car so closely that, in panic, she wrenched the wheel
and her car slewed sideways into the ditch.

As the car crashed down into the ditch there was
a rending, splintering noise; she thought it sounded
as if the end of the world had come. Her windscreen shattered. Glass sprayed everywhere; she instinctively covered her face with her arms,
crouching down in the seat. Luckily, she had been
wearing her seat-belt, or she might have gone head
first through the windscreen and her face would
have been cut to ribbons.

The car rocked wildly, and then settled into the
long grass and weeds. Through her shaking fingers,
Sian saw a splash of red and thought, poppies!—

only to realise after a moment that it was blood on the steering wheel.

My blood! she thought with sick shock. Undoing her seat-belt, she scrambled out on to the road in case there had been a leakage of petrol and an explosion followed. There was no smell of petrol, but she was in a state of panic and wanted to get as far from the car as possible.

The other car hadn't stopped; either the driver hadn't seen her go into the ditch or simply hadn't cared. The lane was empty again; she couldn't hear a sound except the rustle of wild parsley and the melancholy call of birds.

Grabbing her handbag, she set off to walk in search of help. From the map Mrs Cassidy had sent her, the house couldn't be far, indeed, just five minutes away, she came to the high, black, ornately designed ironwork gates set between tall stone posts topped with carved stone gryphons, each bearing a shield.

Shield House. Sian made a face—a pun, she thought grimly, in no mood to be amused by such trifles. The gates stood wide, and at the far end of a meandering drive she saw the large, timbered house with its red-tiled roof. She still had quite a walk ahead of her and she was limping now. Blood was trickling wetly down her face from a cut on her forehead; from flying glass, no doubt. She hadn't bothered to do anything about it—she felt too sick and dizzy, but she set her teeth and doggedly walked on towards the house.

She was almost there when she saw the white sports car again, parked on the drive outside the house. It was empty, but Sian eyed it angrily, trying to hurry because she was afraid she was going to pass out any minute. Who had been driving it just now? It couldn't have been Cass—but it had to be either a member of the family or another guest. Sian had a few things to say to whoever it was, anyway!

A moment later, the front door opened and Cass walked out, tall and lean and casually dressed in an open-necked shirt and cream linen summer trousers. Sian stopped dead and felt odder than ever. He went over to the white sports car and opened the driver's door. It was his car! He must have been driving, after all! How could he drive like a lunatic, force her into a ditch and drive on without even looking back? She was incredulous and appalled; she would have taken bets that it couldn't have been Cass. She had to be wrong about him. What had made her think she knew him well enough to predict how he would behave in any situation?

Serves you right for being so stupid, she told herself, taking another shaky step, and Cass suddenly caught sight of her in his driving-mirror. She saw the flash of those grey eyes in the glass. A second later he was out of the car and running towards her.

'Sian! Sian, my God, what's happened to you?'

He seemed genuinely surprised—she scowled, pushing him away as he tried to put his arms round her. 'You did, damn you!'

'I did?' His face looked almost as bloodless as hers felt. He was staring at her fixedly, and she gave him a defiant glare.

'Just keep your hands to yourself—and stop wavering about!'

'Wavering about? What do you mean?' He came back too quickly for her, and she shook her head, wincing at the way that hurt. 'There's blood all over your head,' Cass said in a strange, thick voice. 'You've had an accident!'

'Oh, you noticed at last,' she bitterly flung at him, narrowing her eyes as she tried to see him clearly. 'I can't take two of you. One of you was bad enough, but two is beyond a joke, especially when neither of you will stand still!'

'I'm standing still,' he said in that strange voice, his arm going round her waist, and this time she didn't push him away, because it was getting much harder for her to stay on her feet. Everything was going round and round as if she was in a washing-machine. No, she thought—a tumble-dryer, I'm in a tumble-dryer.

'What do you mean, a tumble-dryer?' Cass asked, guiding her towards the house. She hadn't realised she was thinking aloud, and giggled.

'I'm sick of you getting inside my head! Stop listening to me think!' She closed her eyes because she felt so sick and it was worse with her eyes open. 'How could you do it?' she asked as she suddenly found herself floating about, weightless.

'Do what?' he asked, oddly close to her, and she frowned.

'Are you inside my head? Is that how you know what I'm thinking?'

She felt his arms tighten, and then it dawned on her that he was carrying her and she had her head on his shoulder. That was why he sounded so close.

'Stop talking and lie still,' he said huskily. 'I'm not inside your head.'

'Why should I believe *you*?' Her voice was scornful. 'Hit-and-run driver!'

'Hit-and-run driver?'

She laughed, wincing again. 'Don't bother to sound so bewildered! I saw the car, even if I didn't see your face. You can't get out of it this time. I'll make sure you pay my garage bill; this isn't going on my insurance, it's going on yours.' Talking so much was exhausting, and she stopped. She felt so strange. So weak and...

The next thing she knew was that she was lying on a bed and a strange man was bending over her. He made soothing noises when she tried to get up, push him away.

'I'm a doctor, just lie still. Everything's OK.'

Sian believed his eyes rather than his voice; she lay still and he lifted her lids and shone lights into her eyes, watching her wince, then he asked questions, and while she answered her eyes roved round the room until they found a familiar object. It turned out to be Cass.

She frowned, looking away. 'I'm fine now, thanks,' she told the doctor, but he smiled politely and shook his head.

'Well, I think we'll have you in hospital tonight for a few tests—you may have concussion. You were only unconscious for a moment, but with head injuries that might not mean much. An X-ray is essential, and some hourly observation. It's lucky I was here.' He straightened and smiled at Cass. 'Even if I am supposed to be off duty!'

'Sorry to find you some work for your spare time!' Cass said lightly, but his eyes were not amused; they were grave. 'I'll drive her to hospital if you'll ring and let them know we're coming. No need for you to come with us, Piers.'

'Well, I'm not a head man or any sort of specialist—but that's a superficial cut on her head; flying glass, I found some in the blood. She probably fainted from shock. I'd be happy to drive her in, though, Cass, just in case I'm wrong and it's more serious than I diagnose.'

'Well, that's up to you,' said Cass.

Sian grimaced from one to the other. 'While you're arguing over who's taking me to hospital, I could be dying from loss of blood.'

'Oh, the cut isn't serious. It just bled a lot.' The doctor was smiling, though.

'Oh, well, what's a few pints of blood?' Sian said drily and both men laughed.

'Nowhere near that much,' said the doctor. 'Blood always looks much worse than it really is. One glass of water and you'll make up for what you lost, and I've stopped the bleeding. There's a bandage on your head.'

'You look very interesting with it,' assured Cass.

'What a comfort!' Sian said, her glance at him hostile. 'While I'm in hospital, perhaps you'll see that my car is pulled out of that ditch and taken to a good garage for repairs.'

He frowned. 'Don't worry about your car.'

'I do worry about it. You may be able to afford to run any number of cars, but I just have one and it costs me the earth just to keep it full of petrol and have it serviced regularly. Repair bills could cripple me, but I meant what I said! You're paying, and you'd better report the accident to the police, too.'

His face was sombre. 'There's no need to involve them. I'll pay all the bills.'

Sian gave him a contemptuous smile, her green eyes icy. 'I had a suspicion you wouldn't want the police informed. Very well. Keep them out of it, but you'd better see to it that I get back my car in tip-top condition.' She sat up gingerly and Cass moved to help. She pushed him away. 'I can manage!'

'I'll carry you!'

'You won't. I can walk.' She put her feet down on the floor and stood up. She still felt a little shaky, but the room wasn't going round and round. Cass hovered, much too close, and she eyed him sideways. 'I'm fine now.'

The doctor stepped nearer and offered his arm. 'Then we'll go down to my car, shall we?'

Cass followed and over her shoulder as they negotiated the stairs Sian said remotely, 'There's no need for you to come to the hospital.'

They moved slowly through a high-vaulted hallway: oak-panelled and fragrant with lavender furniture-polish and summer flowers in great earthenware bowls. Sian was concentrating on walking without that betraying little tremble, but she noted Mrs Cassidy in the background, looking pale and worried. Somewhere there was someone crying; Sian heard that too, although she wondered if she was imagining it. Cass went to speak to his aunt while the doctor helped Sian down the stone steps from the front door. He put her into a comfortable red estate car and she leaned back, closing her eyes briefly, because her head hurt and she still felt weak. The doctor paused before getting behind the wheel; she heard him talking to Cass and felt Cass watching her, but didn't look that way.

Sitting up, she stared ahead of her while the doctor came round the back of the car and got into the seat next to her. The engine came to life and the car drove off with a grate of tyres on gravel. Cass was standing outside the house on the steps, staring after them. She saw him in the wing mirror; his blue striped shirt emphasizing the pallor of his skin and his dark hair blowing around in the wind until he raked it down with one hand in an impatient gesture.

Sian looked away, dry-mouthed and miserable. He wasn't the man she had thought he was. Disillusionment ached inside her as the doctor headed for the black ironwork gates.

'You're a reporter, I gather,' he said, and she started, looking round at him.

'Yes.'

He gave her a brief, wry smile. 'And Magda tells me you're the one who first broke the story about Cass being left at the altar?'

'That's right.' Her voice was defiant; she wasn't apologising for that. She would never feel guilty about Cass again; he had deserved everything that happened to him.

The doctor fell silent, and after a few moments it was Sian who re-started the conversation.

'You're a family friend, not their doctor?'

'I'm both, I hope.' He smiled again, with more warmth.

'I suppose you're Mrs Cassidy's doctor, then?'

He nodded. 'I'm one of the local GPs—we have four at the health care centre a couple of miles away. I'm Piers Brand, by the way—please call me Piers.'

'I'm Sian,' she said, and he smiled.

'I know.'

'How far is it to the hospital?' she asked, and he soothingly told her it was just another five minutes' drive. Sian fell silent and neither spoke until he was pulling in to the casualty department parking bay, when he asked if she felt up to walking into the hospital or should he get a porter with a wheel-chair. Sian said she was quite capable of walking, and he smiled that wry little smile again.

'There's no need to feel you're being asked to prove anything! Nobody will think the less of you if you feel too shaky to walk.'

'But I don't,' she said, and got out of the car without his help, made it into the casualty waiting-room unaided, where she sat while he went off to talk to the nurse on duty at the desk.

Sian was taken off to X-ray, and then saw another doctor who questioned her along much the same lines as the other had; she had lights shone in her eyes, was tested for some fifteen minutes, and then she was told she needn't stay overnight. There seemed to be nothing wrong apart from superficial cuts and bruises; the X-ray had shown no trace of damage.

She wasn't sure if Dr Brand had gone or whether he was waiting for her, but if he wasn't she could always get a taxi. Where to, though? Should she go back to Mrs Cassidy's house? She was reluctant to see Cass again; she was still too angry and shocked

by his hit-and-run driving. Yet if she didn't go back
there it might cause just as much trouble, because
undoubtedly they would come looking for her if
she left the hospital and went back to London.

She walked into the casualty waiting-room, but
Dr Brand wasn't there. Sian's heart constricted,
seeing Cass get to his feet, a newspaper clenched
in one hand.

'They let you go?'

'Were you hoping they'd lock me up for days
and give you a chance to get your clever London
lawyers on the case?' The biting tone of her voice
made him frown.

'Piers has gone. I'll drive you back,' was all he
said, and that made her angrier.

'I suppose you think that if you get me alone you
can talk me into withdrawing the allegation!' she
threw at him, and he took hold of her arm and
hustled her towards the main door of the hospital
so fast that she almost skidded on the highly polished floor. 'Are you trying to kill me?' she muttered, and some nurses going off to supper turned
to stare at them.

Red-faced, Cass snarled, 'Just shut up until we're
in the car!'

'Oh, you'd like that, wouldn't you?' she seethed,
trying to wrench her arm free. 'What do you mean,
anyway? Telling me to shut up! I won't. I'll shout
the truth from the roof if you keep bullying me like
this.'

He dragged her over to where his car was parked.
'Bullying you? Who's bullying you? I just don't
want to have this discussion in front of a horde of
strangers!'

'Witnesses, you mean!' Sian sneered. He yanked the car door open and pushed her into the front passenger seat as if she were a rag doll. As she sprawled there, limp and shaking with rage, he slammed the door and strode round to get in beside her. 'You don't want witnesses, do you?' she accused, and he stared fixedly at her. 'Just as there were no witnesses when you forced my car off the road,' Sian burst out, alarmed by his expression. Those bright, furious eyes were full of threat, but he started the engine and drove off without trying to answer her. She should, perhaps, have held her tongue then. It might have been wiser, not to say safer, but she was in a reckless mood and full of hurt resentment.

'Why did you do it? I thought it was just bad driving at first; you didn't care if I skidded off the road or not! But it was more than that, I think, wasn't it? Otherwise you'd have stopped to make sure I wasn't badly hurt, but you put your foot down and shot away before anyone could get your number. You meant to force me off the road.' She was thinking aloud, rather than actually accusing him. The idea had only just occurred to her, and one part of her mind still didn't believe it. Cass wasn't the murderous type. Or was he?

'You were trying to hurt me,' she said slowly, going white. 'My God, you were trying to kill me!'

CHAPTER EIGHT

'YOU'RE hysterical!' said Cass curtly, his foot down on the accelerator and the car hurtling along at around eighty miles an hour now that they were outside the built-up area surrounding the hospital.

'I'm nothing of the kind! I'm just furious!' snapped Sian, a nervous eye on the speedometer. 'And stop driving so damn fast!'

Hedges flashed by, green meadows were a blur of colour, she saw other drivers staring open-mouthed as they passed them, but Cass didn't slow down for quite a few moments.

'You can't believe anyone tried to kill you! Why should they?' he muttered, and there was something odd in his voice; his face was drawn and frowning. Sian hadn't been talking rationally, she had been using her instincts, and she used them now, watching him and still incredulous over the idea that Cass might have been the driver who forced her off the road and then drove away without stopping.

'Was it you?' she asked huskily, wanting him to deny it, eager to believe him if he said it wasn't true.

He didn't answer, though. He shot her a look and then stared back at the road, brows knit.

Her stomach sank and she felt her eyes burning, as if she was about to cry, but she wouldn't cry over him. She clenched her teeth and fixedly regarded the landscape through which they were driving. It was so calm and tranquil; Sian wished she felt like that, but her mood was stormy and she contrarily wished the weather matched it.

Cass suddenly turned off the road and parked in a leafy lay-by behind which ran a little wood of oak and beech and hazel trees.

Sian shrank back against the seat as he turned to face her. 'Why have you stopped? Start the car. I want to get back.'

'Not until we've talked this out!'

'What is there to talk about? The only talking I should do is to the police!' She gave him an angry smile. 'Don't look so worried—I'm not going to tell them, but I've a damn good mind to put the whole story in the paper!'

'You'll be risking a legal action if you do,' he threatened, his brows black and menacing.

'You wouldn't dare! You know it happened, and if you take legal proceedings that will only prove I'm telling the truth.'

'You think you are, you mean!' he said in furious irony.

'Oh, now you're going to say I imagined it all, I suppose?'

'No, but you're imagining a hell of a lot! Sian, you're intelligent...'

'Thank you! Am I supposed to be flattered enough to forgive and forget?'

'Will you let me finish?' he suddenly shouted, and she jumped, nerves on edge, then glared resentfully at him.

'Don't you shout at me! Who do you think you are?'

'Will you listen for one minute?' He grabbed her shoulders and shook her, and she went into panic. Pulling free, she turned and opened the car door, almost falling out. She didn't wait to see how Cass took that. She started to run, out of the lay-by, into the nearest cover, which happened to be the little wood whose trees crowded the roadside. Sian crashed through the close-set branches, leaves brushing her face, brambles clutching at her clothes, scratching her legs.

Behind her, she heard the slam of the driver's door and the running thud of feet which meant Cass was pursuing her. She was in such a state of wild tension that she almost sobbed, her breathing thick and tortured. Running faster, she dived deeper into the shadowy woodland, through green ferns, the dappled light from above flickering all around her and making her head ache.

Cass caught up with her in a little hollow full of towering beech, the earth beneath them deep with leaf-mould from years of autumn falls. Sian felt his hands descend on her arms and struggled, shaking, until he spun her to face him, and as she looked up at him, breathlessly protesting, he bent his head and took her mouth with bruising force.

She could have struggled, but she didn't. She was so angry that she met the kiss on tiptoe, her mouth as full of fury as his. They kissed in an act of war, then his arms went round her and held her punishingly tightly, and her arms went round his neck and her hands closed on his hair, winding it round her fingers, pulling it, clutching it ruthlessly. Her rage burned out on his lips, and she winced at the consuming violence of his hands as they roved over her, but when at last their mouths parted in sheer exhaustion, she was breathing as if she had run a marathon, and Cass almost staggered back until he could lean against a beech trunk, still holding her, like a man rescuing a drowning victim who is himself almost dead when he crawls on to dry land.

They looked at each other dazedly.

'Damn you!' Sian whispered with her last scrap of energy.

His mouth went crooked; he looked down wryly and took a series of gasping breaths. 'You're driving me mad,' he said, and she was shaken, her face flushing hotly. He laughed, watching her. 'Are you going to listen to me now?'

'Say what you like, I'm too tired to argue,' she muttered, trying to free herself.

He wouldn't allow it; his hands tightened and she gave up, letting her body lean slackly on him since he wouldn't let her stand by herself. Let him take her weight, then, until she could find the strength to get away.

'You aren't thinking, Sian,' he said flatly. 'Why should I deliberately force you off the road?'

'That's obvious! Because it was me who helped Annette run away from you, and then made the headlines with the story of how you got left at the altar!'

His mouth twisted and his eyes were steel bright. 'OK, I wasn't very happy about that...'

'You hated me for it! Your ego couldn't take the humiliation.'

'My ego is a lot tougher than you seem to think!'

The dry tone made her pause and laugh. 'That's certainly true!' His ego was dented, perhaps, but she had never been able to believe that he was so crazy about Annette that her flight had hurt him deeply or wrecked his sense of identity. He was too assured, too successful; if any man had a firm idea of himself, it was William Cassidy. A girl like Annette couldn't destroy that self-image, although she must have hurt his pride.

'And I didn't hate you,' he said softly, and she looked quickly away, a funny little tremor running through her. 'I didn't deliberately force you off the road, either,' Cass went on, watching her in a way she found disturbing. 'That was an accident. Bad driving, I'm afraid, and I'm sorry. I'll make it up to you—we don't need legal interference, do we? You can trust me. Name the compensation you want and it's yours. Of course, your car will be replaced—a new one, you can pick it out yourself.'

'Bribery now,' Sian thought, aloud, her green eyes speculative and slanting sideways to watch him. 'What exactly is going on? What are you hiding?'

'Don't let that imagination of yours loose again!'

She pushed his hands down and this time he let go of her, his face hard and wary.

'Were you really driving that car?' she demanded.

He hesitated and she stiffened. 'Look, can we drop the subject?' he asked, turning away. 'I think we should get back—you must be dead on your feet. This has been quite a difficult evening for you and you ought to be resting, not running about a wood in the dark.'

It wasn't dark yet, although the twilight had gathered thickly enough to give his face a shadowy menace. Sian couldn't see him well enough now to tell what he was really thinking, but she was sure he was playing some complicated game with her; there was sleight of hand here, although she wasn't certain how or why.

'And if it wasn't you, who was it?' she persisted, and he sighed heavily.

'Sian! Drop it!'

'I'm getting warm, am I? How close am I?'

There was a silence; she could almost hear him thinking, even if she couldn't see his face.

'Not nearly close enough,' he said suddenly, his voice mocking, and his arms went round her again before she could evade them.

'You're not distracting me again!' she muttered, turning her head aside.

'Why not? You've been distracting me for days. I can hardly keep my mind on anything else when you're around.'

'Except Annette, of course!' Sian murmured bitterly.

'Can we leave Annette out of it?' he frowned.

'Hardly! You were going to marry her just the other day. I realise how you must feel, but I can't say I find it flattering that you keep making passes at me to stop yourself thinking about her!'

'I didn't say I was doing that!'

'You didn't have to!'

'Oh, you read my mind, did you?'

'I don't know about your mind—but I can tell when a man really fancies me, and when he's using me as a stand-in for another woman, and I don't like it!' She broke free again and began to walk back to the car, feeling suddenly tired and weak-legged. She swayed slightly, and at once Cass caught up with her and put his arm right round her.

'Lean on me. You're a crazy girl, do you know that? Haven't you had enough drama for one evening? Why did you run off like that?'

'Shut up,' she muttered, stumbling over a fallen branch on the path.

Cass halted her with one hand and a second later had lifted her over his shoulder in a fireman's lift, as if she were a sack of potatoes.

Sian gave a cry of wordless protest, and he slapped her lightly on the behind. 'You're in no state to walk, so stop arguing!'

He was right, but she gave him a token kick in the ribs, all the same, and heard him grunt in surprise.

'What was that for? I'm only trying to help you, and if you had a shred of honesty you'd admit I was right.'

'Why do you think I kicked you? I hate people who are always so sure they're right, even when they are!'

He laughed shortly then. 'I don't think I'll ever understand what makes you tick! You're a mystery to me, but then, most women are incomprehensible to most men.'

He gently deposited her in the car and they drove off through the falling night. Sian closed her eyes and half drowsed, in a drained state of sleepy contentment. It was only as they drove up towards his aunt's house that she realised that he had successfully put a stop to her questions about the car crash.

Mrs Cassidy met them on the front steps of her home. 'My dear Sian, this is terrible! Are you sure you're well enough to leave hospital? You look so pale. I can't tell you how sorry I am! I blame myself.'

'It wasn't your fault.' Sian smiled wearily at her.

'But you were a guest in my house! I apologise, for my whole family!'

Sian looked hard at her, then at Cass, whose face was blank.

'OK,' he said curtly. 'Now we've got that out of the way, shall we get her to bed before she passes out again?'

His aunt said with dignity, 'Of course, right away, but I wanted to apologise before anything else.'

'Thank you,' Sian said, smiling at her again.

'I'll take you up to your room.' Mrs Cassidy turned towards the stairs.

'Oh, my luggage was in my car!' Sian paused, frowning, and Cass said quietly, 'I had it taken out. It's in your room now. And your car is at the local garage, being repaired.'

'Thanks.' She followed his aunt without looking his way again.

'Are you hungry, my dear? What would you like to eat? It can be sent up to your room—an omelette? Or...'

'Omelette would be wonderful,' Sian said, quite hungry now that she actually thought about it.

'I'll order it right away.' Mrs Cassidy opened a door. 'I hope this room is comfortable enough for you. Why don't you get into bed and I'll send up your supper at once, so that you can get to sleep quickly. You're sure a meal won't keep you awake? I couldn't eat at this hour, but when I was young I remember I had a cast-iron digestion—what about you?'

Sian laughed. 'I think I'll sleep tonight, whatever I eat! I could sleep on a clothes-line after the day I've had!'

The older woman's face clouded over again. 'Yes, I'm sure. When I think what could have happened! Why, you might have been killed! I'm so appalled, my dear. That one of my own family could do such a thing!'

Sian tensed, watching her intently, but at that moment Mrs Cassidy glanced back and they both saw Cass on the top stair, watching them, listening. Mrs Cassidy excused herself and went back to join him, and Sian wryly closed the bedroom door.

The room was enchanting: a very feminine room with delicate pink curtains, a silver-shot cream wallpaper, a pink carpet and a modern four-poster bed with floor-length curtains of white gauze. The bed-linen was just as delightful: a lace bedspread over a pink broderie anglaise duvet cover and lace-frilled pink pillows. Sian went into the en-suite bathroom and changed into her nightdress after washing, and inspecting her dramatically bandaged head. She noted wryly that she was looking distinctly pale and interesting, but she no longer had a headache.

She had just climbed into bed when there was a knock at her door. 'Come in!' she called, and then felt a jab of alarm when she saw Cass walking towards her. 'What do you want?' she asked, stiffening against the high-piled pillows, before she noticed the tray he carried. She had been too busy looking at his face to see what he had in his hands.

'Your omelette.' He deftly adjusted the tray which suddenly had hinged legs which fitted neatly over Sian's lap on the bed, turning the tray into a table.

'How clever!' she commented as he whisked a silver cover off to reveal the golden half-moon of the omelette.

'My aunt's housekeeper filled it with tomatoes and mushrooms and herbs,' he said as she eyed the plate.

'It looks delicious. Thank you.'

'I'll be back for the tray later—would you like coffee? Or would it keep you awake?'

'No, I don't think I'd better drink coffee,' she said, wishing he wouldn't keep looking at her. Her nightdress was too revealing; her bare shoulders and throat seemed to fascinate him, and Sian felt like pulling the sheet up to her chin, but that would be to admit she found his gaze disturbing, and she wasn't going to do that. She didn't want him to know he had any effect on her at all.

He nodded and vanished, and she gave a long sigh of relief.

The omelette was as delicious as it looked. Sian ate it slowly, drank some of the chilled milk that had been sent up with it, then leaned back on the pillows and closed her eyes, yawning.

'Sleepy?'

His voice made her start; her lids flew up and she blinked to find him so close, inches away, although she hadn't heard him come into the room. He sat down on the side of the bed and her colour rose hectically. She looked aside, afraid of looking into his eyes.

'Very. It's been a long day.'

'How do you feel?' he asked, pushing aside a clinging strand of blonde hair which was hiding the bandage on her forehead.

'OK, thanks.' Sian felt him staring at her head, but kept her lashes lowered, wishing he would go.

'I hope you won't have a scar there.' Cass brushed the hairs back over the bandage, then slowly ran his hand down over her head, making a little shiver pass through her. 'Cold?' he asked, his fingers lightly stroking along her bare shoulder.

'I want to go to sleep,' she huskily said. 'Goodnight.'

'You ate the omelette—was it good?' He took no notice of her hint.

'Very, thank you. I enjoyed it.' He was gently playing with the lace-trimmed strap of her nightdress, pushing it down over her arm and up again, and Sian was nervously aware of everything he did.

'This room is perfect for you,' he murmured. 'All pink and silver, and your nightdress matches exactly, as if you'd known.'

'Your aunt will wonder what you're doing in here,' Sian said desperately, pushing his hand away as it strayed lower and his fingertips softly trailed over her half-covered breast.

'My aunt has gone to bed.' He bent closer and his lips touched the curve of her shoulder; it wasn't so much a kiss as the butterfly brush of a wing, gone almost before she had felt it, yet the impact of it made her gasp and, on a reflex action, close her eyes.

'Don't!' she whispered, trembling.

'You're quite a puzzle, Sian,' he said. 'Brisk career girl one minute, and then you sit there looking like a little girl and acting as though you'd never been kissed in your life! Every time I think I'm getting to know you, you pull another surprise on me—another rabbit comes out of the hat! I can see I won't be bored while you're around.'

Sian hid her smile, her head turned aside. 'I don't say I'm bored, Mr Cassidy, but would you mind leaving so that I can get some sleep?'

He laughed softly. 'Sometimes there's a touch of the cat about you, too! Quite a complex mixture, in fact.'

'Goodnight,' Sian insisted, and he got up, the bed springs making a squeaking protest.

'Goodnight, Sian,' he said, and bent quickly before she had warning of his intention. His mouth was warm and possessive; there was nothing tentative about the kiss, it was given with command and assurance, even though it didn't linger. Sian heard him collect the tray from the floor where she had placed it before he had come back, then he was gone, the door closing quietly.

She opened her eyes and the room seemed lonely, far too empty. She threw several pillows to the end of the bed and turned out the light before lying down with just one pillow under her head. Cass had said she was a puzzle, but he was just as bewildering to her. She wished she knew how he really felt about Annette. Why had he asked her to marry him? And had it been him driving the white sports car, or was he covering up for someone else?

Sian had picked up hints, clues—she suspected it might have been his sister, Magdalena, but why should Magdalena have forced her off the road, then driven on deliberately, leaving her in the ditch?

What grievance did Magdalena have against her? Presumably the same one Cass had—that she had helped Annette, then printed the story in the newspaper she worked for! Sian could understand why Cass might be burning with secret rage about that, and even understood that his sister could be very upset too, but surely Magdalena couldn't be angry enough to risk killing a total stranger? If Sian went to the police, Magdalena would be charged with hit-and-run driving, and face a stiff penalty. Would she have been so stupid? Come to that, of course, the same applied to Cass, but Sian found it increasingly hard to believe he would have left her. It wasn't in character.

She slept very late next day, and only woke up when hammering started in the garden. At first, Sian wove the noise into her dreams and made it the crash of her heart in panic as she ran from some nebulous terror; then, as she began to wake, she thought her head was thudding as it had just after the accident. It was only when she opened her eyes and saw the strange room that she fully surfaced to remember where she was and what had happened. She lay there, staring around, one hand going up to her forehead to finger the bandage. Her head no longer hurt. She felt quite normal—except that she was saturated with sleep, heavy and stupid with it. She had been dreaming all night; fragments of strange dreams littered her memory, but when she tried to make sense of them she failed.

Cass had been in them. That much she was sure about. Cass had been in them all!

She pushed that aside hurriedly; she didn't want to think about Cass. Getting slowly out of bed, she stretched, lazy as a cat, then went to the window. Pulling the curtain aside, she warily peered out, but there was no sign of Cass or any of his family. There were people in the garden, all strangers, workmen in overalls and dungarees, in shirt-sleeves and jeans. They were putting up a giant green canvas tent on the billiard-table smooth lawn. Others were erecting stalls nearby. The hammering came from one big man without a shirt at all who was driving the tent-pegs into the ground, wielding a hammer as big as himself.

Sian dropped the curtain back into place and went to run a bath, then looked through the clothes she had brought in her case. She laid a choice out on the bed and went into the bathroom to take a leisurely soak in the foamy water. It was half an hour before she emerged, smelling of musk and flowers, her naked body wrapped in an enormous pink bath towel.

She opened the door to find herself face to face with Cass, inches away from her. He grinned, eyes mocking as they drifted downwards to view the whole of her.

'I was just about to knock!'

'What are you doing in my room?' she bristled, flushed.

'I brought you some breakfast!'

She followed the gesture of his hand and saw the tray on her bed, biting her lip with self-irritation. 'Oh. Thanks.'

'I thought it was time you woke up,' he drawled, shooting back his cuff to show her the face of his watch.

'Gone eleven! I'd no idea it was that late! I'm sorry, you should have woken me!'

'You needed the sleep. Did you sleep well?'

She nodded, self-consciously aware that her shoulders were bare and the towel a very inadequate protection against roving eyes. It had become damp now, and clung to her body like a second skin.

'What's under the silver cover?' She bent to lift it from the plate on the tray and felt her stomach clamour at the sight of food. 'Oh, gorgeous! Bacon, mushrooms, tomatoes... I mustn't let it get cold, so I'd better dress quickly and start eating!'

He grinned at her, grey eyes teasing. 'Is that a hint?'

She smiled back drily. 'Well, what do you think?'

He strolled to the door. 'OK, when you've eaten, come down and meet some of my friends, will you?'

Sian threw a look of consternation after him, but before she could answer he had gone, closing the door after him. Some of his friends? she thought with a sinking in her stomach. What was he up to now?

She was so perturbed that she had no real appetite once she sat down to eat the breakfast he had brought up. She tried some of it, ate some toast, drank some orange juice and some coffee, then she finished doing her make-up, her hands not too steady.

She had chosen a dress of pleated cotton with a tight waist, scooped neckline and full, swirling skirt.

The misty lavender-blue shade suited her, and she loved the plaited silver belt. She had picked plaited silver sandals to match it, and had given her eyelids a lavender shadow with the same silvery sheen as that on a moth's wing.

She ruefully considered herself reflected in the dressing-table mirror. The soft romanticism of the dress, the belt, the silver shoes, were hardly sexy or exciting. Men weren't going to stop in their tracks or gasp, were they?

'So what?' she asked herself. 'Who are you trying to bowl over?' Then she turned away hurriedly and made for the door, before stopping and going back for her breakfast tray.

As she reached the bottom of the stairs, she met a young girl in a green wrap-around overall who smiled, said cheerfully, 'Morning!' although it must almost be midday by now, and then took the tray from her.

'Thank you,' Sian said, and would have gone on to ask where she could find Mrs Cassidy, but at the sound of her voice Cass himself appeared in the doorway of a room across the hall.

'Ah, there you are! Come and meet my family.'

In some trepidation, Sian slowly joined him, flushing at the way his grey eyes wandered over her.

'You look lovely,' he said softly, and she lowered her eyes because she didn't want him to know the compliment had taken her breath away.

It was a while before she could say huskily, 'Thank you.' She had been paid many compliments before, by all sorts of men, for all sorts of reasons, from the terse, 'Not bad work!' she sometimes got from Leo, and treasured, to the practised insincerity of the office flirts telling her they really fancied her when they didn't, but merely wanted to coax her out on a date because they knew she would turn them down and that made her a challenge they couldn't pass by. No other man had ever made her feel weak inside at the way he looked at her, or made her feel she could walk on air because of something he had said.

I'm in love with him, she thought, then angrily told herself she was crazy: how on earth could you be in love on such short acquaintance?

He somehow had a strange power over her re-actions, that much she couldn't deny. He caused all sorts of weird things to happen to her body; to her heart and lungs, her pulses and nerves, the blood circulating in her veins, her very skin. He was a drug to which she was wildly susceptible; just a little of him and she was having some dangerous symptoms, but that didn't add up to love, or to anything long-term, let alone permanent.

He held out his hand with a faintly imperious gesture. 'Come in, then! You aren't shy, are you?' She should have ignored both his hand and his teasing voice, but while she was deciding what to do he caught hold of her and pulled her into the room.

Sian's nervous eyes flashed around, receiving an impression of green and ivory: cool, light, spring-like. The sitting-room was spacious and sunlit, with comfortable furniture, gently faded brocades at windows, a deep, soft carpet underfoot. This was both an elegant room and a family room—there were valuable and pretty porcelain figures every-where, but also silver-framed photographs of children and dogs; an antique French clock stood next to a vase of wild flowers obviously crammed into place in a haphazard fashion, both of these standing on what Sian suspected to be a priceless Chippendale table.

It wasn't the room that made her nervous, though; it was the people in it, all staring at her with what she felt were hostile eyes.

Mrs Cassidy at least, smiled, patting the sofa she sat on. 'Come and sit next to me, my dear. How do you feel this morning? Did you sleep well?'

'Yes, thank you,' said Sian, walking a little unsteadily as she crossed the room, because those unfriendly eyes were unnerving. There were four other people in the room—two strange men, an unfamiliar but very attractive girl, in a pink dress—and Magdalena.

It was Magdalena who radiated hostility, of course, and as Sian sat down she made herself look at the other girl, challenging her, the way she would have stared back at a threatening dog in her path. Sian wasn't going to be scared off or put down by Magdalena, but she was puzzled by that overt hostility. What had she ever done to Magdalena, for heaven's sake, that warranted these black looks?

CHAPTER NINE

CASS interrupted her thoughts by introducing the others. 'Sian, I don't think you've met my brother, Malcolm, have you?'

'Hello,' she said as the thin, dark young man smiled at her. He had a certain resemblance to Cass, but he lacked that visible aura of power. He seemed quiet and shy and a little unsure of himself, although he was quite attractive in his way, and the girl with him was very pretty indeed.

Cass introduced her, too. 'Andrea Hill, a friend of Malcolm's.'

Sian smiled; Andrea half smiled back, but with reserve. Sian got the impression that she knew all about the situation, and was firmly on the side of the Cassidy family. Andrea had possessive eyes and a determined jaw; she slid her hand into Malcolm's arm as if to make it clear he was her property. Malcolm, interestingly, looked startled; a bird taken by surprise by a cat.

'You know my sister, of course,' Cass murmured. Before Sian could look at Magdalena, he added, 'And this is her husband, Robert Shaw.'

Sian switched her smile to the third man, who began to smile back, then stopped as his wife turned angry eyes on him.

'Magda!' Cass said ominously, and she looked at her brother, biting her lip and scowling like a sulky child.

'Magda has something to say to you,' Mrs Cassidy chimed in suddenly, but Magda seemed in no hurry to say it.

'Malcolm, why don't you and Andrea go and check on the workmen?' Cass suggested. 'They should have finished by now, but I can still hear hammering.'

Andrea was in no hurry to be dragged away from this interesting conversation, but under those cool grey eyes she didn't quite have the nerve to stay. Cass was a very different proposition from his brother, and Malcolm was already on his way to the door, so Andrea had to go with him. When the door had closed behind them, Cass looked back at his sister encouragingly, one brow raised.

Magdalena swirled round suddenly to face Sian; she shot one look at her, then looked down. Very flushed, she burst out, as if in accusation, 'It was me driving the car, not Cass!'

'Oh, I see,' Sian said, not knowing quite how to respond, then there was a silence.

'And...' prompted Cass in a firm voice, watching his sister, not Sian.

'And I apologise,' Magda said through her teeth, looking up then, and eyeing Sian with hatred.

'Magda!' Cass said, but this time she ignored him. Turning on her heel, she ran out of the room, slamming the door.

Her husband sighed. 'I'll go and talk to her.' He looked rather sheepishly at Sian. 'Sorry about this, she shouldn't have...she has this temper, and when she loses it she does stupid things.'

He went out and Mrs Cassidy groaned. 'What are we going to do with that girl? Cass, should I go too? Poor Robert can't handle her, he gives in to her too much.' She got up without waiting for an answer. 'I'll make her come back and do it properly this time?'

'No, please don't,' Sian said, appalled at the idea.

'Oh, I think she should,' Mrs Cassidy insisted at the door. 'She really must learn not to do such dreadful things. She thinks she can get away with anything, and one day she may do something really terrible. She could have killed you. I'm sure she didn't mean to, and I'm sure the whole episode has frightened her, but she can't be allowed just to get away with it. Not this time. She must face up to what she did.'

She went out and Sian stared at the window, watching the green sway of ivy on the wall, the dance of the wind through a maple tree at the edge of the lawns. Cass stood watching her, and she was very conscious of his nearness.

'I'm afraid Magda was spoilt,' he said. 'The only girl, and she was delicate as a child—we all spoiled her, from my father down. Robert adores her, too, he never denies her anything. She has grown up thinking she can do just as she likes.'

'Why didn't you tell me before?' Sian asked, still bewildered. She had said such terrible things to him; why hadn't he made her believe it wasn't him who had driven the white car?

'I did,' he said flatly. 'You didn't believe me.'

'You didn't really try to make me!' She thought back over the scene in the little wood, flushed and appalled by what she had said to him. 'You looked guilty!'

'Maybe that was because I felt guilty,' he said, his voice weary.

'Why should you, if it wasn't you?'

'She's my sister.' He prowled up and down, his hands in his pockets, his dark head bent. 'I suppose I felt responsible for what she'd done.' She saw his sombre face from an odd angle and watched him gravely. What was he thinking? There was a silence which lengthened, making her uneasy; she breathed carefully, afraid of breaking the mood. It was so quiet in the room.

'Magda was spoilt too early. She's always been unstable, given to these outbursts. She's possessive and jealous—she was jealous of Annette when they were both small, because my father made rather a pet of Annette, who was born just before Magda. My father wanted a little girl badly, and Annette was pretty and rather shy; even after Magda arrived, Dad went on giving Annette presents now and then, and as Magda grew up she resented that. She once got hold of a big doll Dad had bought for Annette. Magda smashed its head into a wall and stamped on the pieces.'

Sian drew a shocked breath. 'My God! That's crazy...'

Cass frowned. 'No, she isn't crazy—Dad thought she might be sick. He took her to a psychiatrist, but the specialist said she was just very spoilt and self-obsessed. He said it was perfectly normal for a child to be jealous if a parent showed fondness for another child, and it can be very hard if the other child is a sibling, let alone someone who isn't part of the family.'

'I'm sure that's true, but children grow out of it!'

He sighed, his grey eyes intent on her. 'Yes, exactly—but Magda has never learnt discipline, she doesn't hide what she feels, the way most of us learn to do. That's one of the differences between children and adults, isn't it? That when we're small we can't hide our feelings, but when we grow up we cover up all the time.'

He was looking into her eyes and she felt her colour rising, a hot pulse beating in her neck. Was he still talking about Magda, or was he talking on two levels at once? There was a mocking irony in his stare and he was smiling crookedly—or was she imagining that?

'Forcing another car off the road isn't a piece of childish bad behaviour!' Sian protested, hurriedly walking to the window to keep her back to him.

'No.' His voice was hard. 'Don't worry, Magda isn't going to get away with it. Why do you think she confessed just now? We've all made it very clear that she has gone beyond the limit and that she has got to take some treatment again. The trouble is, she's perfectly OK except for this one area, this almost paranoid jealousy.'

'But why me? Why should she be jealous of me?' Sian kept her eyes on the garden; watching the people moving about on the green lawns. The green canvas marquee was up, the stalls were being hung with flags and women were hurrying about with boxes of things to be put out for sale. Large tubs and troughs of summer flowers had been placed here and there, to give the right festive air, and Sian tried to be interested, but was only really aware of Cass behind her.

'She thought you were bringing Annette here!' he said brusquely.

Sian spun, green eyes wide. 'Why should she think that?'

'Nobody had told her that my aunt had invited you, and when she spotted you in the car ahead, for some reason she decided you had Annette with you, you were bringing her back. She said she was afraid the wedding was on again, and so...'

'And you say she isn't crazy?' Sian broke out, and he winced, his eyes a frozen wasteland.

'I've said, she must see a psychiatrist. She does have a problem.'

'You say that far too casually,' Sian said with an incredulous stare. 'Don't you realise that if I'd reported the accident to the police, she could be facing a serious charge today?'

'Of course I realise it!' he said with impatience, catching her eye and looking hurriedly away.

Suspicion hit Sian. She watched him, frowning, her mind working like an overheated engine. 'Is that why you didn't tell me that it wasn't you?'

It was a shot in the dark, but it hit its target. His face tightened, a dark flush rose in his cheeks.

'It was...' she whispered, shaken. He had let her go on believing that it had been him in the white car because he hoped she wouldn't go to the police and inform on *him*. And that meant only one thing—Cass had been gambling that he meant something to her.

And he won, hadn't he? Sian stood there rigidly, white-faced, hating him. It was humiliating to know that he was so sure of her feelings for him.

'Sian,' he said, catching her arms and bending to kiss her, but she pushed him away.

'Don't you come near me again, not ever!'

'I'm sorry, Sian. I didn't want to hurt you!'

'Sorry?' The word was an insult; her voice shook. 'You don't know the meaning of the word!'

'Do you think I wanted you to believe I could do a thing like that?' He was getting angry, too, his voice vibrating with harsh feeling. 'I tried to tell you the truth, but you wouldn't believe me.'

'You didn't try very hard, though, did you?'

'If you knew anything about me, you would have known I wasn't capable of a thing like that!' He turned icy eyes on her, his mouth curling.

'But you were capable of using what I thought to get your sister off the hook!' she spat out, and saw his eyes flash. 'You could have convinced me if you really tried, but you didn't care what I thought!'

'I cared,' he said through his teeth, and tried to take hold of her again.

'Oh, sure you did!' Sian muttered, slapping his hands away. 'Don't try to touch me, or I'll hit you so hard you won't get up for a week!'

He eyed her ominously. 'Don't threaten me, Sian.'

'Then stay away from me!'

'I just want to tell you the truth!'

'The truth? You?' She laughed and his brows twitched together, black and heavy.

'Yes, damn you! The truth! Do you think I was flattered when I realised you thought I was a hit-and-run driver?' His voice seared her, harsh and burning with sudden rage. She flinched away, frowning.

'You had an option! You could have told me I'd made a mistake!'

'At first I was too shaken. Insulted, incredulous—not to mention as angry as hell. It all happened too fast, then you went off to hospital with Piers and I talked to Magda and realised she'd deliberately run you off the road. I didn't know what to do, but I was afraid of the police coming into it because that might push her right over the edge. Her grasp on reality isn't too strong.' He paused, hesitating. 'And she's my little sister,' he added flatly. 'I have to take care of her, whatever she's done.'

Sian understood that, and couldn't think of anything to say in response. After all, he hardly knew her—but Magda *was* his sister! Of course he had chosen to defend Magda, however much he hurt *her*.

'Then why have you told me now?' she asked. 'Why not let me go on thinking it was you?'

'Magda has to face up to what she did; she has to admit it and take the blame, or else she'll do something like that again—even worse, maybe! She can't be allowed to think she has some sort of immunity, can do as she likes.' He sounded stern, remote, and Sian shivered. His reason for telling the truth, then, had nothing to do with *her*; he was still concerned only with his sister.

'I still don't think you realise what might have happened!' she accused, and he looked down at her, his eyes brilliant with anger.

'Of course I realise! Whenever I think that you could have been killed I feel sick...'

She wished she could believe the feeling in his eyes, but she dared not trust him any more. There was too much hidden between them; too many question marks in her mind.

'And it wasn't even me she wanted to kill!' She met his eyes and saw them flick away, as they always did at the mention of Annette—the biggest question mark of all. Something else occurred to Sian then, and she frowned, watching him closely.

'If you knew she hated Annette, why were you going to marry...?' She broke off the question because she didn't think she could stand hearing him talking about Annette; she didn't want to know any more. He must have been deeply in love with her, or he wouldn't have risked marrying someone his sister hated that much. Or hadn't he realised until too late that Magda still hated Annette like poison?

He wasn't answering her, anyway; he was staring at nothing, his face in hard profile.

Sian made for the door suddenly. 'I'm going for a walk in the garden!'

He followed. 'I'll show you the roses and the croquet lawn—can you play? We could have a game. They've set it up so that people can play this afternoon. They're charging them, of course—it's all for charity, everything is being done to make money.'

Sian didn't look round at him. 'I'd rather be alone,' she said in a stiff, cold voice, then began to run, and this time he didn't follow.

It was a relief to be out of the house, in the sunlight, although she found herself surrounded by people at first. Workmen, ladies with armfuls of books, junk, plants which they were heaping up on the stalls, children setting up a crazy golf course on one lawn, while in another corner some boys were arranging coconuts on battered wooden cups for a coconut shy. She felt people looking at her, curious eyes following her. No doubt they wondered who she was—but she ignored them all, making for the distant part of the garden she could see: a wilder area of trees, rough grass, shrubs. At least there she could be alone to think.

One group of women discussed her so loudly that she could hear every word, and maybe was meant to! 'Is it her?' one asked.

Another said, 'No, she isn't old enough. The pictures in the papers made her look thirty, at least, and this one can't be more than twenty-five.'

Sian wanted to run, to get away from the speculative eyes, the faintly malicious voices, but she made herself walk steadily, her eyes fixed on nothing.

'I think it is her,' someone else said.

'Well, I don't think much of his taste! The other one was better-looking.'

'Men like blondes, though, don't they?'

Sian was almost out of earshot; the last words floated to her on the summer air, making her grind her teeth. What made people think that blonde hair meant there was nothing underneath the scalp? Why did people think in stereotypes?

The stuff of my trade, she thought cynically as she slowed down among the trees. Among them she saw a white ironwork seat against a swag of rich pink clematis, the flowers spilling down behind it from an old half-dead apple tree which looked as if it had been struck by lightning and no longer fruited.

Sian made for it and sat down sideways, her knees clasped by her two hands and her feet on the end of the seat, propped on the elegant curled ironwork armrest.

Cass was a ruthless man. He had used her without scruple whenever he felt it necessary—to distract the media from Annette, or in covering up what his sister had done. It didn't bother him that she might have been badly hurt by believing that it had been he who had forced her off the road and then driven on without stopping.

Did that mean he had no idea she was falling in love with him? Or merely that he knew, yet was still prepared to use her feelings for his own purposes without caring what that did to her?

She closed her eyes, then angrily opened them again and pulled a swathe of clematis towards her; she fingered one flower, played with the petals unthinkingly, shredding them and letting them fall lightly on the long grass—soft, velvety, pink drifts among the whiskery stems.

He was a mystery, a shadowed maze into which she had wandered, in which she was lost. She didn't understand him at all, nor did she think he wanted her to!

She ought to leave now, right away, without seeing him again. Why had he been going to marry Annette? Sian found it increasingly difficult to believe he had ever been in love. He didn't act like a man in love; he had made passes at her ever since they had met; and when he talked about Annette he didn't sound like a man in love. Sian heard more genuine excitement in his voice when he talked to her. In fact, he spoke about Annette kindly, patiently, as if she were a child he was responsible for—even his fury over her flight had not been quite in keeping with the way a jilted bridegroom would feel. It had been more the exasperation of someone who has been made to look a fool in public, and he had pursued her to bring her back only for her father's sake. Had he seen her since the day he'd driven Sian back to London from the hospital? Had he tried to see her? If he had, he hadn't mentioned it, but then, he was a secretive man who never mentioned anything if he could avoid it.

A movement among the trees made her stiffen and look round, expecting to see Cass and steeling herself to send him away.

It was a man hovering there, watching her among the leafy branches, but it wasn't Cass. For an instant Sian had a primitive flash of terror. She was alone and the unknown seemed sinister.

Then he came out into the sunlight of the little glade, and with a start of incredulity she recognised him.

'Louis?'

'Hello,' he said, strolling over, very London-dressed in a smooth pale grey suit with a pink shirt and a grey tie slashed with pink stripes. He looked totally out of place, totally wrong.

'What on earth are you doing here?' Sian asked.

'You don't seem too pleased to see me!' His voice had the familiar petulant ring, but she was long past the stage of placating him and she answered shortly.

'I don't know why you're here. I wasn't expecting to see you.'

'I'm not sure why I'm here myself—curiosity, I suppose.' He picked up her feet and held her legs up while he sat down on the seat beside her, lowering her legs again over his lap. Sian would have swung them free, but he held them firmly, one hand stroking along her calf.

'What do you think you're doing?' she said, struggling to break free, but then he took her breath away.

'When the invitation came, I almost threw it in the bin.'

'Invitation?' Sian gave him a startled look.

'From your editor... what's-his-name.'

'Leo?'

'That's it, Leo. Funny chap; what is he up to, anyway?'

'Leo sent you an invitation? To what?' she patiently persisted, and he gave a querulous sigh.

'To this garden party, of course!' he said, and Sian's eyes rounded in disbelief.

'He doesn't have the right to hand out invitations, and anyway, I don't think you need an invitation, it's a public event to raise money for charity.'

'But there are tickets to get in—and the press were given some free ones. Complimentaries. He sent me one of those.'

'Leo sent you a complimentary?'

He eyed her shrewdly, his hand wandering up and down her leg, because Sian had been too dumbfounded to notice what he was doing for some time. 'You never used to be this slow-thinking. What's happened to you lately? Your brain seems to have gone to seed. It must be all this mixing with the rich and famous; it's finally got to you.'

'Why on earth would Leo do that?' Sian slowly thought aloud, and Louis gave her a teasing grin.

'Isn't it obvious? He was mischief-making—what else? Heaven alone knows what he expected to happen, but I can tell when someone's hoping to cause trouble, and that's that he was doing. I just wondered why—is he afraid he'll lose the best girl reporter in Fleet Street, or something?'

The malice didn't bother her, nor did the sideways, satisfied look. Louis could be as sarcastic as he liked, make what fun he liked, he didn't bother her at all. She was over him, he meant nothing to her now, but she was annoyed with Leo. She knew her editor and his childish glee when he made the cauldron bubble, and that was, as Louis had just said, undoubtedly what he had hoped to do by sending Louis here. He wanted to stir up a storm, create a dramatic story for the paper. Cass had only wanted the media to swallow what *he* handed them; Leo was ruthless. He wanted to plant his own story with the ingredients he chose. He was quite cheerful about using her; like Cass! Were all men like that? Well, this time neither Cass nor Leo was doing it to her, not if she could stop it.

'Never mind what Leo wants, you aren't stopping,' she told Louis.

He raised his brows. 'I'm not getting orders, am I, darling? Because I don't take orders from my women.'

'I'm not one of your women, Louis, not any more.' She thought about it, then added angrily, 'And I never was!'

Maybe that was a tactical mistake, because his face darkened and he took on that familiar look of petulance. She had wounded his male pride, his precious ego.

'Weren't you, then?' he asked, and she tried to get up hurriedly, alarmed by his expression, but he reached up and caught her waist and yanked her backwards over his lap. She couldn't stop herself falling. He started kissing her hard while she was still off balance, her head back over the iron armrest, her blonde hair spilling into the long grass. Sian fought him furiously, biting his lower lip until he gave a cry of rage and pain, his head shooting up.

'You little bitch!'

He fingered his mouth, which was bleeding. 'Blood,' he said, stupefied by the sight of it on his finger. 'Look what you did!'

Sian couldn't stay angry in the face of that incredulous, injured expression. She began to giggle.

That was when they both heard a rustling, the crack of a twig underfoot. Louis hurriedly looked across the clearing and went a funny shade of puce.

The next minute Sian was on the ground and rolling away, and Louis was on his feet, running. Sian scrambled up, ruefully rubbing her behind, laughing, but her laughter stopped as she looked up into Cass's face. It was leaping with black rage and there was no humour in it anywhere.

CHAPTER TEN

'So it isn't over, after all?' Cass's voice was congested, thick with rage or something else, and Sian stood there, staring at him, her nerves prickling as if she were in some sort of danger.

'Yes, it is,' she began.

'Don't lie to me!' he suddenly yelled.

She almost jumped out of her skin, and then grew angry too. 'Don't you shout at me!' she yelled back.

'I don't like being lied to!' he muttered, coming a step nearer. 'You told me last time we saw him that he was just an old flame—but obviously he's still burning.'

She sighed, shaking her head. 'Look, this is none of your business, but I *was* telling the truth—there's nothing between me and Louis any more.'

'No?' he sneered. 'Is that why I saw you sprawling all over him? And the two of you had been making love. Don't tell me you hadn't, because your lipstick is smudged to hell, and I saw it on his mouth.' His own mouth twisted in distaste and his eyes were contemptuous. Sian winced, hurt by that look, but then wondered why she should put up with having him talk to her, look at her, like that!

'What right do you think you have...' she began, but he talked on over her.

'And I'd like to know how he got in here; there are supposed to be security men on the gate. I'll have a few sharp words to say to them later! This is private property.'

'And so am I!' Sian said furiously, very red. 'My own property—nobody else's! Who the hell do you think you are, talking to me like this?' He stood there, listening, watching her with an odd, uncertain, almost puzzled look on his face, and she shouted at him, 'I don't have to explain myself to you, Mr William Cassidy, and I won't put up with being bullied.'

'Why did you lie to me? That's all I want to know,' Cass muttered, glaring down at her.

'I didn't.' He was much too close. He was making her light-headed merely by standing there, those grey eyes brilliant, that mouth pure temptation.

'I suppose you're telling me that there's something wrong with my eyesight! That I didn't see you lying across him, that he didn't have your lipstick on his mouth!' He had calmed down a fraction, but only because he had turned icy, his tone biting with sarcasm, and she curled her hands into fists, wishing she dared hit him, but afraid to take the risk because Cass was capable of hitting her back, and in this mood she thought he probably would!

'He grabbed me,' she admitted brusquely. 'I didn't want him to!'

Cass laughed; well, it was supposed to be laughter, but it sounded pretty unamused, a harsh bark of disbelief.

'Oh, of course!'

'And it wasn't my lipstick on his mouth—it was blood. His, where I bit him when he tried to kiss me!'

His brows pulled together, and he stared at her mouth, which contrarily began to quiver, although she tried to stiffen it.

'Now you come to mention it, your lipstick is more a pale pink shade, and that *was* red on his mouth!'

'My lipstick is lavender-pink, to be accurate!' Sian said coldly, turning to go, but Cass caught hold of her shoulder and spun her round again.

'But you still haven't explained what he was doing in my aunt's garden and how he got in!'

'He had an invitation to the garden party—and I've no idea why he was allowed through the gates before the party started. You'd have to ask him.'

'An invitation?' Cass scowled blackly again. 'From you?'

'My editor passed on to him one of the complimentary tickets your aunt sent the newspaper.' Sian gave him a barbed smile. 'Well, it was *your* idea to invite the press. *Your* idea that I should be here so that they could write about us! You get what you pay for in this world, and Leo was only doing what comes naturally to a tabloid editor!'

'Is that guy a reporter, then?'

She shook her head and he stared speculatively, watching the colour deepen in her face as he thought aloud. 'So if he doesn't work for your paper, why should your editor have given him a ticket? Shall I guess? Hoping to provoke a scene? Get a more dramatic story for your paper? What was he hoping I'd do, I wonder? Shoot the guy? Throw him in the pond? Or just beat him up?'

Sian laughed. 'Something like that. Editors have very simple minds, and they like their gossip colourful.'

'What a pity I saw you two when I did,' Cass drawled. 'If you hadn't sneaked in here to meet your old flame in private...'

'I didn't! There were too many people around the gardens, so I came here to be alone, but Louis must have seen me and followed me in here. I had no idea he was here; Leo didn't tell me what he planned.'

Cass considered her drily and her green eyes met his, her face serious. He put his hand on her bare arm and a little shiver ran down her spine.

'There have been too many people around ever since I met you,' Cass said softly. 'I haven't had a real chance to get you alone.' Her breath caught and she looked down, her lashes brushing her cheek. 'It's just as well I didn't catch you with the old flame in public, or I hate to think what I might have done,' he said, his fingertips sliding caressingly up and down her skin. 'When I saw you two just now, I was so jealous I wanted to kill you.'

She shook her head fiercely, tears burning behind her lids. 'Don't...'

'Don't what, Sian?' he murmured, his voice hardening.

'Say things you don't mean.'

'I mean them. Why should you think I'd say them if I didn't?' He sounded baffled, uneasy.

'What about Annette?' she cried, voice shaky.

'Ah,' he said on a long sigh. 'Annette.'

'Nobody gets over loving someone that quickly!' Sian whispered, a tear trickling out from under her lid.

'Darling!' Cass said on a deep, shaken sound, and then his lips were on her wet eyes and his arms round her, and Sian ached to let herself yield weakly

to the comfort of his strength, but she wouldn't—
she pushed at his shoulders and turned her face
away from those hunting lips.

'Do I have to bite you, too?'

Cass laughed, surprised. 'Termagant! I believe
you would.'

'You'd better believe it!' she said firmly, but she
didn't meet his eyes as he let go of her, because he
would be able to read too much in her eyes and it
would be dangerous to let Cass know how he made
her feel. She hadn't believed it possible to feel
emotion like this; the painful, burning intensity was
a shock to her, utterly new and bewildering. She
had had men friends ever since she'd left school at
eighteen, she had even thought she might be in love
once or twice; she had suffered when relationships
broke up, but she had never quite been able to give
herself completely to anyone else. She had always
had reservations, held back a part of herself that
was essential, the core of her own being. She had
thought it would always be like that; she had come
to think she wasn't capable of a really intense
emotion, but that was what she was feeling now.
It had never happened like this before. Her whole
body seemed raw, as if she were haemorrhaging in-
ternally at the very idea of ever saying goodbye to
Cass.

Cass backed and sat down on the ironwork
bench. 'Then we'd better talk.'

She stayed where she was, eyes lowered, the curve
of her face stubborn. 'Talk away.'

'Come and sit down!'

It wasn't so much a suggestion or request as an
order, autocratically given, and Sian stayed at a
distance, grimacing.

'I'm fine where I am. I've already had one hand-to-hand combat on that bench. I can do without a repeat performance.'

He laughed shortly. 'Don't worry, I'll keep my hands to myself, but I'm not sitting here while you stand, so please sit down!'

'Oh, well, if you say please,' Sian said, deliberately provocative, and took a seat at the far end of the bench.

He eyed her sideways. 'Are you always this irritating?'

'Always.'

'I feel quite sorry for myself,' Cass murmured, and her colour rose again, but she kept her face averted, hoping he wouldn't notice.

'Can we get on with this, please?'

He sat sideways, facing her, his arm sliding along the bench, but his hand didn't actually touch her, just lay nearby, his fingers tapping on the back of the ironwork.

'When my mother died it left my father very lonely, but he wouldn't marry again, partly for Magda's sake, because she was very jealous and clinging even then, and he was afraid of what it might do to her if he remarried. After a while, though, he decided she needed female companionship, other girls to talk to, older women looking after her, so he sent her to a good girls' school. She hated boarding, but Dad insisted, although he missed her and he was alone even more. While she was away at school, he visited Annette's home several times a week, sometimes more often. He thought of Annette as another daughter, in some ways. He used to say to me that I must marry her when she grew up, so that she could really be his daughter.'

Sian looked incredulously at him. 'You aren't going to tell me you proposed to her simply to please your father?'

He laughed. 'Nothing that simple, no, but in a way he planted the idea in my head years ago. Annette was just a little girl then. I didn't take him seriously, and I don't think he meant it seriously either. But when Dad died and Magda got married and Malcolm looked as if he might be going to get engaged too any day, I suddenly felt lonely, the way Dad had been when our mother died. There I was in that big house, and half the time I seemed to be alone. I was working very hard and I was often too tired to go out in the evenings. At weekends it wasn't so bad, but even if I did go out with a girl after work I caught myself yawning, and they didn't like that much.'

'I'm sure!' Sian said, laughing.

He watched her, his grey eyes gleaming softly. 'I love it when you laugh like that; your whole face lights up.'

Sian stopped laughing and looked down, her throat dry. 'Go on with your story.'

'You wouldn't put any of this in your paper, would you?' he asked with a rueful note which meant that he didn't really believe she would.

'No,' Sian said, and he smiled; she watched through her lowered lashes and ached with passion. It hurt to love this much; she wished she had never stopped that day to pick up the runaway bride, she should have driven on and ignored her. She wouldn't now feel this need and pain if she had.

'I'm not trying to say there weren't girls, that's the point,' Cass said. 'But none of them mattered, and gradually I got sick of the way I was living. I had brief relationships, the girls were nice and usually pretty, but somehow it wasn't important whether I saw them again or not, and the house seemed empty at night. I would wake up sometimes and listen to the silence and feel so lonely. Then Annette started work with me, and she was such a link with my father, with life the way it had been before Dad died and the family started splitting up. At first I just felt comfortable with her. I took her out to dinner if she worked late with me—I'd never have asked any of my other secretaries out because I'd have been afraid they would get ideas and that would ruin our working relationship. But I didn't feel I had to worry about Annette; she was like another sister. So I saw a lot of her and it was fun spoiling her, giving her presents, taking her to expensive places just to see her face. She was still half a child in some ways. I think I was copying my father, doing what he had done. I didn't set out to; it was instinctive, I wasn't really aware what I was doing.'

'You were falling in love with her,' Sian said huskily, swallowing on the jab of pain she felt.

'No,' he said, and she looked up then, eyes wide, angry.

'Now who's lying? Of course you must have been.'

He shook his head. 'I never thought I was in love with her. I knew what I felt, what in a way I still feel—affection, nostalgia, a desire to look after someone rather helpless. She was still more of a sister than a lover, and when I knew her father had a bad heart I decided that marriage would be an answer for both of us. I wouldn't come home to an empty, silent house every night after Malcolm married—and Annette wouldn't be left alone in the world when her father died. I'd no idea, you see, that there was another man. She'd never breathed a word, to me or her father. I thought she was lonely, too. I had got to the age when you don't believe you'll ever feel anything world-shattering. I'd never met that one woman and I didn't think I ever would. But I was very fond of Annette, and we had our lives in common; we'd always known each other on that casual, day-to-day basis, and it seemed to me that that was what marriage turned into once the honeymoon period was over. I thought Annette and I were at the stage most married couples reach after a while; we had merely skipped the first stage, and I didn't think that mattered.'

Sian considered him with incredulity and laughter. 'You're crazy, do you know that?'

He slid along the seat and his hand touched her cheek. 'I know that. I learnt it from you, even though you're crazy too.'

She was so happy, she felt she was floating, and to tether herself down she caught hold of his hand and pulled it down from her face, held it tightly.

'I must be crazy to listen to this.'

'*You're* world-shattering!' Cass said, so close now that his mouth was moving against her ear, his breathing warm on her skin.

'Stop that. I don't know if I want to get involved with a lunatic.'

'A lover and a poet,' he murmured, his voice husky with amusement and another, much deeper feeling. 'I never thought I'd sink to the level of writing poetry, of course, but for you I might even do that.'

'I'd insist on it,' Sian said, putting a hand up to push away his head. It obstinately stayed where it was, his face buried in her throat, and she absently found herself stroking his thick, dark hair. 'If I were stupid enough to consider getting involved with you, that is, which of course, I'm not.'

'Aren't you, darling?' His mouth was hot and urgent on her neck; the words came out thickly, barely audible except to someone who was intensely concentrated on everything he did and said.

'If you weren't in love with Annette, why were you so violent when she ran away from you?' she asked, having difficulty ignoring what he was doing, but determined to get the whole truth.

'She left me standing at the altar. Of course I was furious. Who wouldn't be? But I wasn't maddened by love. I felt more like slapping her, to be frank, until her father had the heart attack, and after that I just wanted to find her and get her to the hospital in time.' He gently bit her earlobe.

Sian curled the warm strands of hair around her fingers. 'So it was just your ego that was hurt?' She tried to yank his head back, but it wouldn't budge.

'What do you mean, *just* my ego? Why do you think the Japanese are so set on never losing face? Nobody likes looking a fool, and there's no joke so funny as the bridegroom left standing at the altar, except, of course, the bride left standing there!'

'That wouldn't be funny!' Sian thought aloud, grimacing.

'There you are, then. Music-hall jokes to most people, but if it's you in that situation the joke isn't so funny, even if you aren't actually in love.' He put a hand under her chin and forced her head back so that she had to look up at him.

Green eyes wide and shimmering with a mixture of happiness and passion, Sian stared back as he searched her face with that intent gaze.

'Sian?' His voice was unsure, husky. 'Will you listen now? I'm in love. How about you?'

'I don't know,' she wailed, afraid to admit that what she felt was anything so serious.

Cass watched her lips; they trembled under his stare and he leaned over to kiss them, softly at first, coaxing a response, experimenting gently, and then with a rapidly mounting excitement and desire that swept them both away. He had both arms around her and pulled her on to his lap; she wound her arms around him and kissed him back urgently, no longer trying to hold back or disguise what she felt. There was a terrible sense of relief as she let go of her defences, giving in with hunger and yearning and a driving sense of need.

Cass groaned her name, his arms tightening around her. He was breathing thickly; she could hear his heart crashing inside his ribs with an almost frightening violence, and her own heart beat far too fast. Her blood was overheating until she was burning up, but they went on kissing, touching each other with hands that shook, both of them oblivious to everything around them.

It was the cry of a bird overhead that made them come out of it. Sian jumped, her eyes opening wide, drowning in passion. Cass looked down at her with a dazed expression, his face dark red and his eyes glittering.

She laid her head against him, breathing roughly. 'I feel as if I've just run a marathon.'

He cradled her on his lap, in his arms, his head on her hair. 'That's odd. So do I. Maybe we did?'

She gave a little gurgle of laughter. 'Where are we? I can't remember.'

'In the garden; hear the birds?'

'That was it—a bird calling, that was what made me wake up.'

'Were you asleep? I don't like the sound of that. When I make love to you I want you wide awake.' He kissed her hair and tried to move his lips down over her face, but she laughed and evaded him.

'Be serious for a moment.'

'I am serious, about you,' he whispered and she believed him then, her heart hurting inside her. 'I love you, Sian. How about you?' he said again, as he had said before he'd kissed her, and this time she didn't say she didn't know, because she did and she was no longer afraid to admit it.

'I love you,' she said huskily and he sighed.

'Darling.' He held her in a happy silence, their bodies close and warm.

Sian listened to the other sounds rising above the quiet rhythms of the garden, above the call of birds, the rustle of leaves, the whisper of the grass. People were all over the place out there; she could hear some sort of brass band tuning up, hear someone testing a loudspeaker, hear voices urgently calling one to the other as the last arrangements for the garden party were put into effect.

'We don't have to go out there and get stared at, do we?' She couldn't bear the idea of strangers staring, listening to them talking to each other, guessing at how they felt. It was all so new to her even now; she felt like someone with a delicate globe of crystal in her hands which might smash if it wasn't handled with care.

'We don't have to do anything you don't want to do, darling,' he said, stroking her sleek blonde hair with a tender hand.

'Could we be naughty and escape before the party starts?'

'What about your own dear colleagues? We'll be disappointing them.' He sounded amused and she laughed.

'Won't that be too bad!'

'Your editor will want to tear you limb from limb. Not that I'd let him, of course.' He laughed softly, his hand deftly travelling. 'Such beautiful limbs; no one but me shall touch them.'

Sian looked through her lashes, mocking him. 'It was you who invited the press here and who wanted to distract them from Annette—I don't care what Leo says. He'll get over it! By tomorrow he'll be obsessed with another story. Nothing lasts in our world. Why do you think they call it the *news*? Because it has to be as hot as new bread, the very latest story. Yesterday's news is history—and we don't print history. Our readers want their gossip up to the minute.' She half closed her eyes as his hand delicately touched her breast. 'That's nice, but not here or now. I don't want to read about this in tomorrow's paper, if you don't mind.'

'The biter bit,' he drily commented, letting her sit up on the seat and smiling at her. 'Now you know how all your own victims felt.'

'I keep telling you, I'm not a gossip columnist. I'm strictly a news reporter, a very different animal. I cover facts, not bedroom whispers.' She looked at her watch and frowned. 'If we're to get away before we're trapped by the press, we'd better go soon. Look at the time!'

Cass pulled her to her feet. 'My car is parked in the old stableyard at the side of the house, right away from the gardens where the party is being held. If we go through these trees we can run across to the yard in two minutes, and once we're at my car we can get away easily enough.'

'Another chase!' Sian said ruefully, making a face. 'Ever since the day I picked Annette up, I seem to have spent most of my time running away from someone or other. Well, one last time won't kill me, I suppose.'

Cass had been smiling as she talked, but he suddenly sobered, staring at her in a frowning way. 'Oh, God, yes,' he said inexplicably. 'Sian, how do you feel about weddings?'

Bewildered, she flushed. 'Weddings?'

'Do you want a white one with all the fuss and trimmings, I mean? Your family and friends, and mine, and a big reception—all that?'

'Are you proposing?' She was breathless again and laughing. 'Cass, really! Aren't you rushing things a bit? Give me time to...'

'Don't you see?' he interrupted grimly. 'I couldn't go through all that again. I'd have nightmares about it happening again; being left at the altar, all the newspapers gleefully hashing up what happened this time, people laughing...'

'Cass, I wouldn't do that to you,' she said gently, touching his face. 'Stop thinking about it. We have all the time in the world to get to know one another. Don't start fretting over something that won't happen—and anyway, if you don't want a white wedding we'll elope. That would be more fun, anyway. We needn't tell another soul, just go away and telegrams later.' She laughed. 'I'd like it best that way, wouldn't you? No hassle, no problems, just us against the world.'

'Yes,' he said huskily, taking her hand and kissing the palm. 'Just us against the world.'

'If I decide to marry you,' Sian reminded him. 'I haven't even started to think about it yet.'

'Start now,' he said, kissing the fast-beating blue vein at her wrist.

'If we don't go soon, we won't get out of here alive,' said Sian breathlessly, and Cass took her hand tightly in his, and they ran together through the trees, across some grass into the stableyard where his car was parked. As they drove out of the gates, Sian saw some old friends from Fleet Street strolling lazily into the garden party. One of them caught sight of her in the car and his head swung, his jaw dropped. He began to run back to his own car, but Cass put his foot down and they shot away too fast for pursuit. Sian laughed.

'I think we'll find ourselves in the gossip columns tomorrow, anyway. Will you mind?'

'At the moment, I don't really mind about anything,' Cass said. 'You've had five minutes to think over my proposal—made up your mind yet?'

'Don't rush me!' she said plaintively, but of course he did.

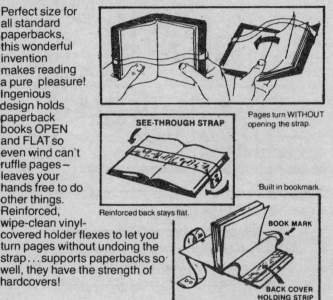